THE GREAT ART CAPER

Harriet wuz Here

Victoria Jamieson

Henry Holt and Company
NEW YORK

Chapter 1

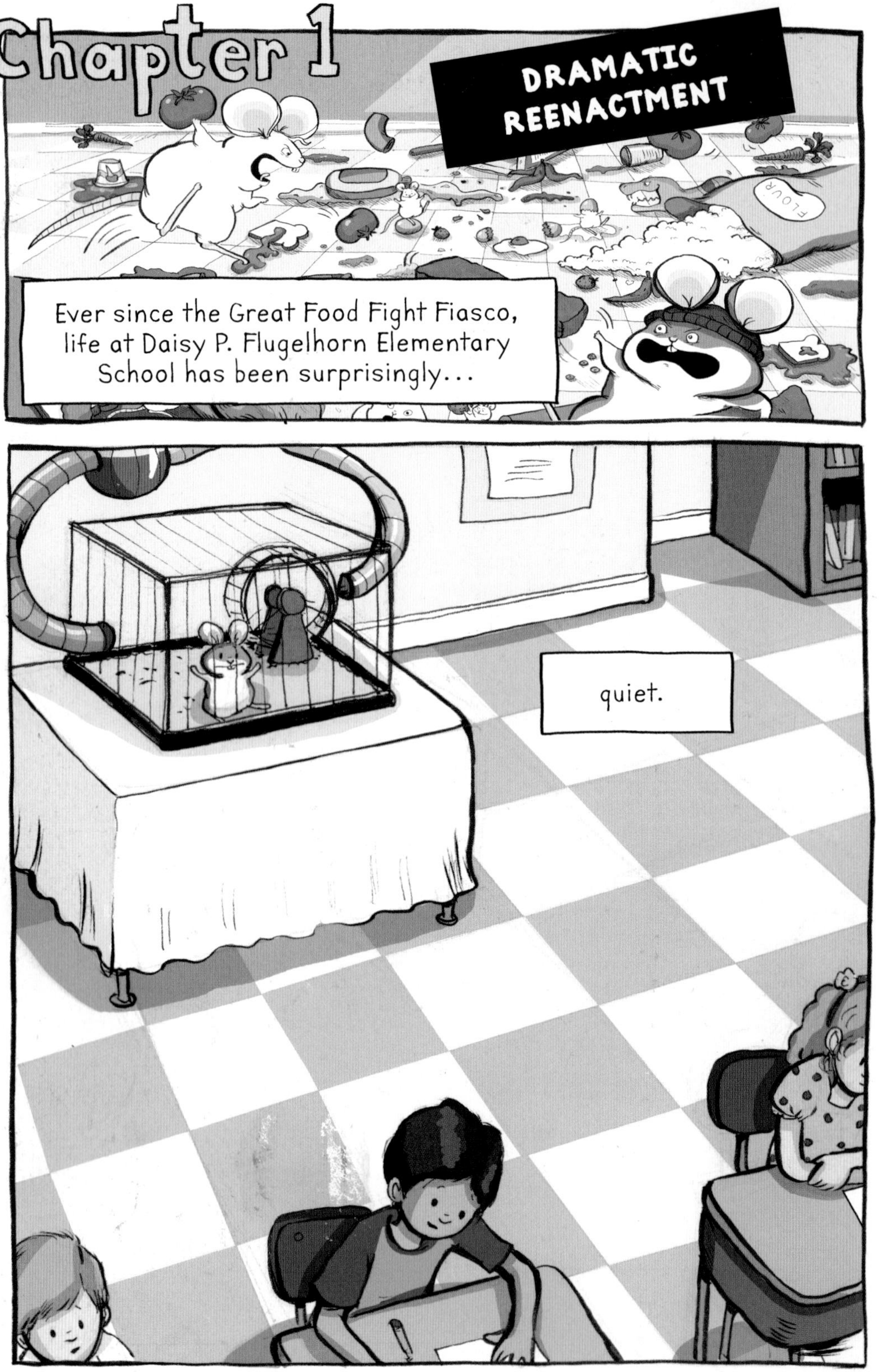

DRAMATIC REENACTMENT
FLOUR
Ever since the Great Food Fight Fiasco, life at Daisy P. Flugelhorn Elementary School has been surprisingly...
quiet.

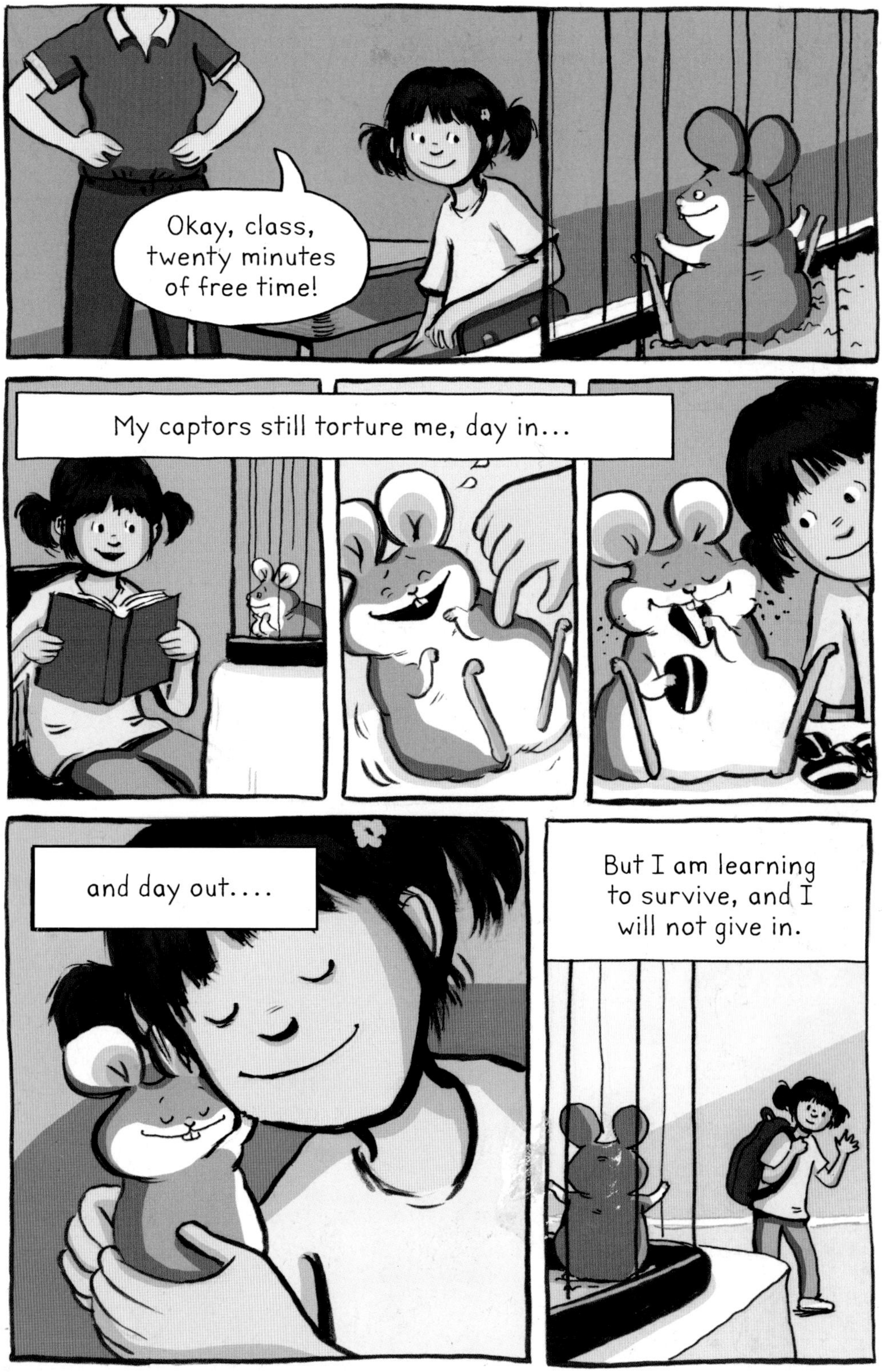
Okay, class, twenty minutes of free time!
My captors still torture me, day in...
and day out....
But I am learning to survive, and I will not give in.

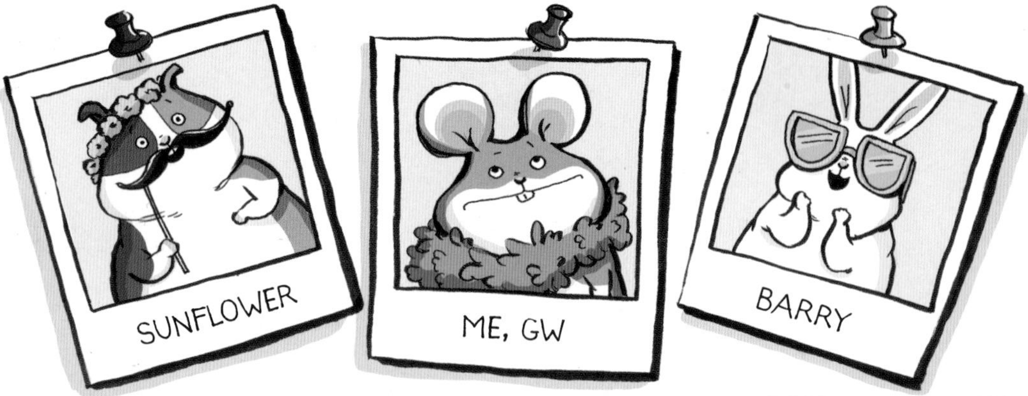
SUNFLOWER
ME, GW
BARRY

The Furry Fiends still meet up in the kindergarten classroom almost every night, but without any great battles to fight, our meetings have become somewhat tame.

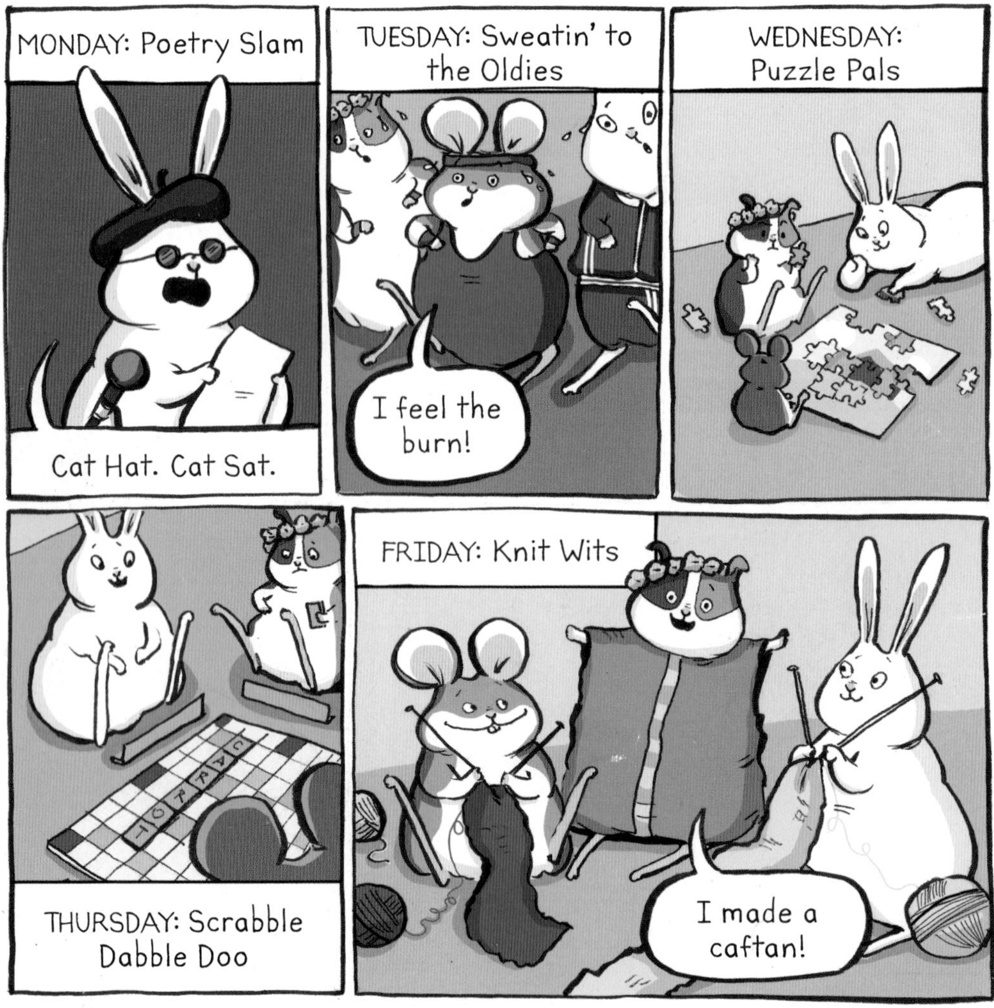
MONDAY: Poetry Slam
Cat Hat. Cat Sat.
TUESDAY: Sweatin' to the Oldies
I feel the burn!
WEDNESDAY: Puzzle Pals
THURSDAY: Scrabble Dabble Doo
FRIDAY: Knit Wits
I made a caftan!

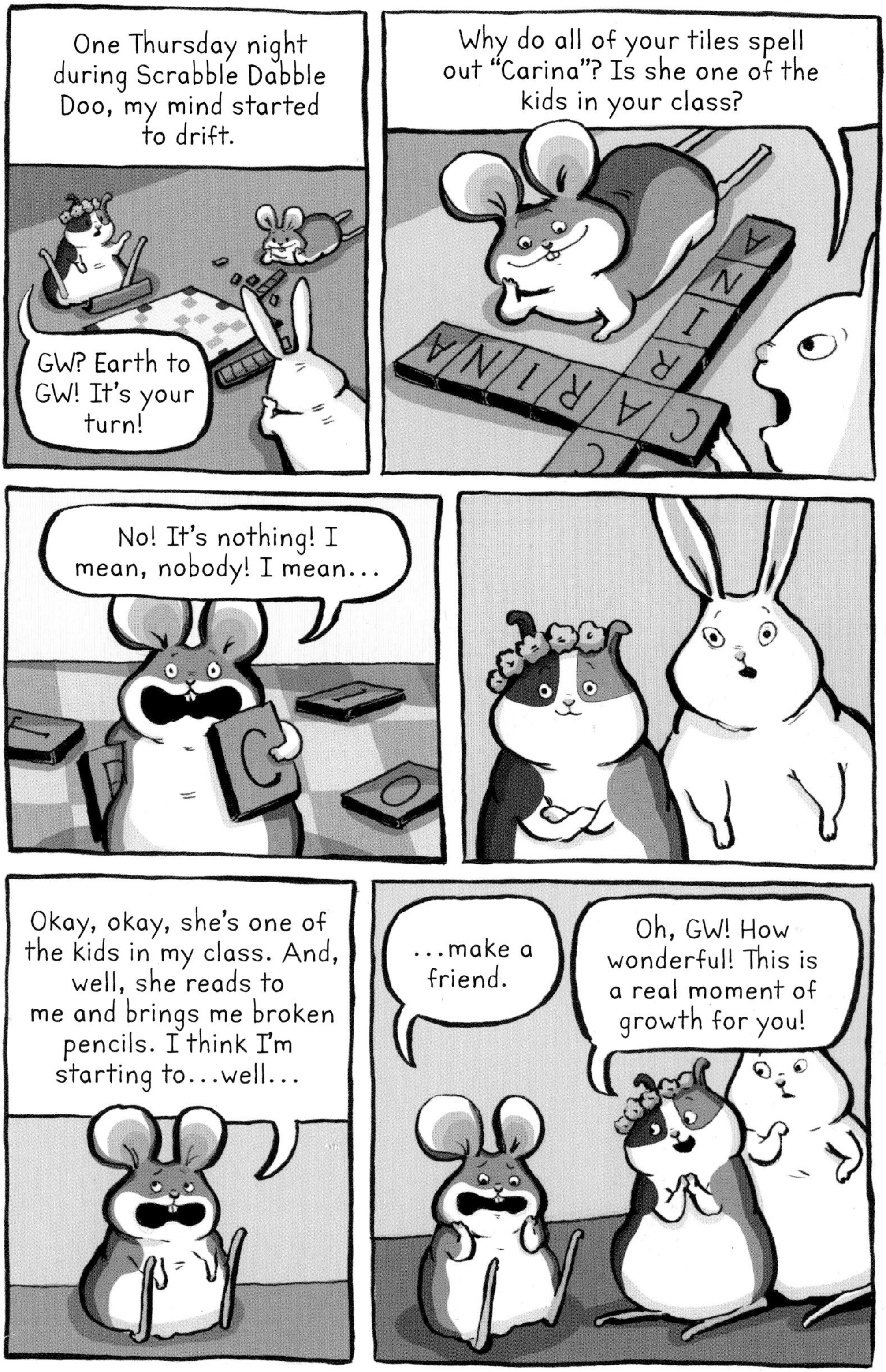

One Thursday night during Scrabble Dabble Doo, my mind started to drift.
GW? Earth to GW! It's your turn!
Why do all of your tiles spell out "Carina"? Is she one of the kids in your class?
CARINA
CARINA
No! It's nothing! I mean, nobody! I mean...
Okay, okay, she's one of the kids in my class. And, well, she reads to me and brings me broken pencils. I think I'm starting to...well...
...make a friend.
Oh, GW! How wonderful! This is a real moment of growth for you!

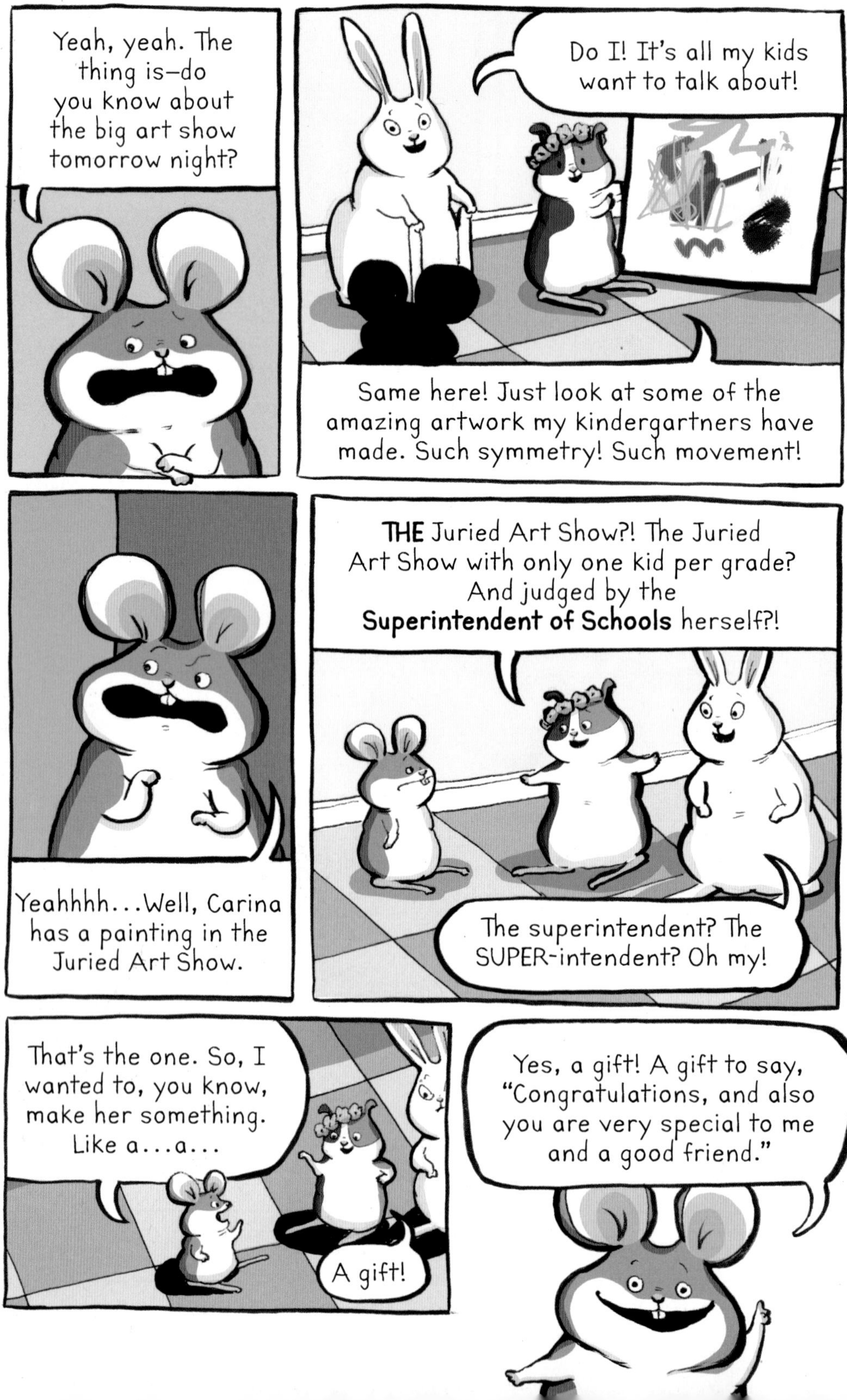
Yeah, yeah. The thing is—do you know about the big art show tomorrow night?
Do I! It's all my kids want to talk about!
Same here! Just look at some of the amazing artwork my kindergartners have made. Such symmetry! Such movement!
Yeahhhh...Well, Carina has a painting in the Juried Art Show.
THE Juried Art Show?! The Juried Art Show with only one kid per grade? And judged by the **Superintendent of Schools** herself?!
The superintendent? The SUPER-intendent? Oh my!
That's the one. So, I wanted to, you know, make her something. Like a...a...
A gift!
Yes, a gift! A gift to say, "Congratulations, and also you are very special to me and a good friend."

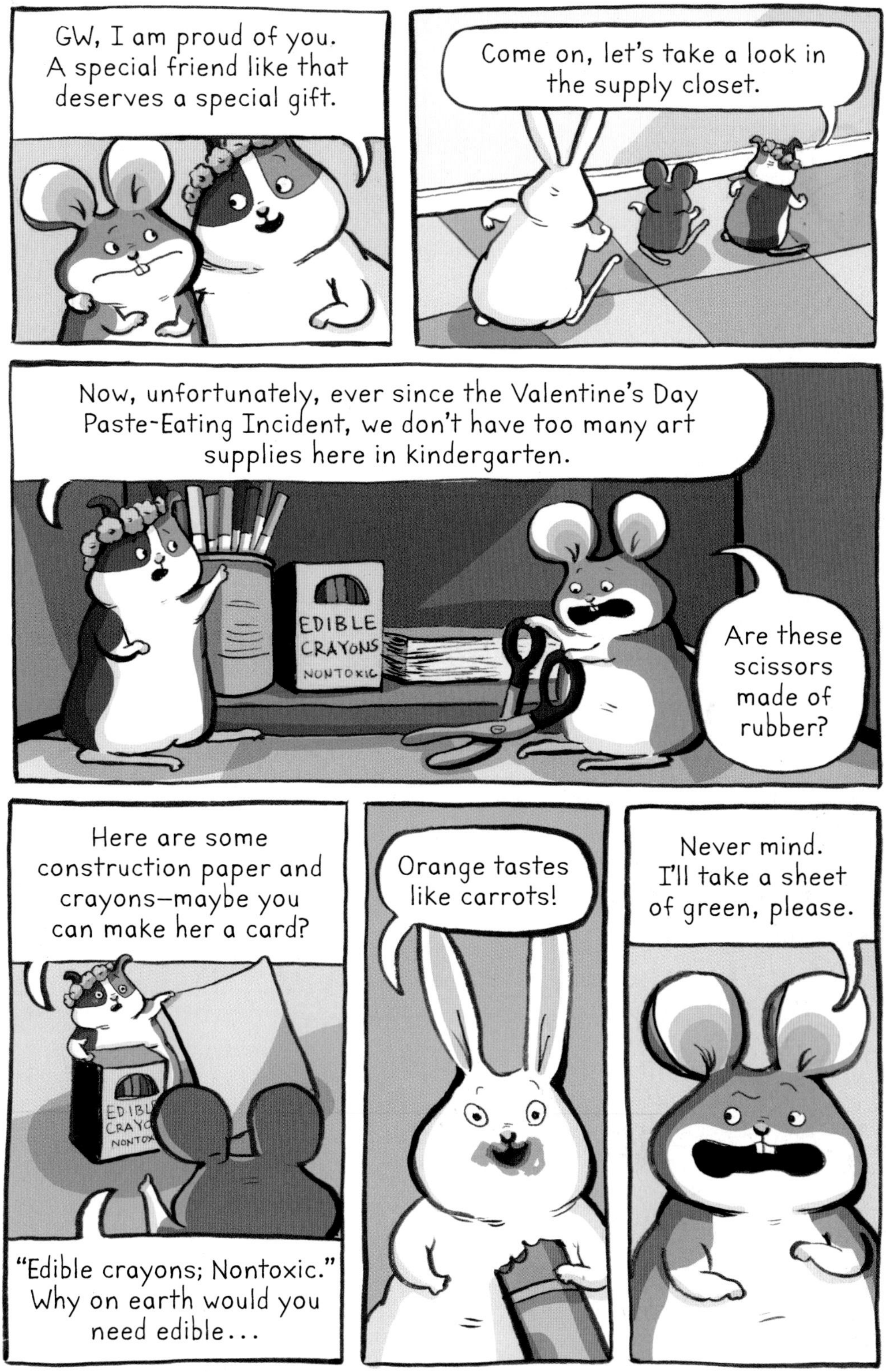
GW, I am proud of you. A special friend like that deserves a special gift.
Come on, let's take a look in the supply closet.
Now, unfortunately, ever since the Valentine's Day Paste-Eating Incident, we don't have too many art supplies here in kindergarten.
EDIBLE CRAYONS NONTOXIC
Are these scissors made of rubber?
Here are some construction paper and crayons—maybe you can make her a card?
"Edible crayons; Nontoxic." Why on earth would you need edible...
Orange tastes like carrots!
Never mind. I'll take a sheet of green, please.

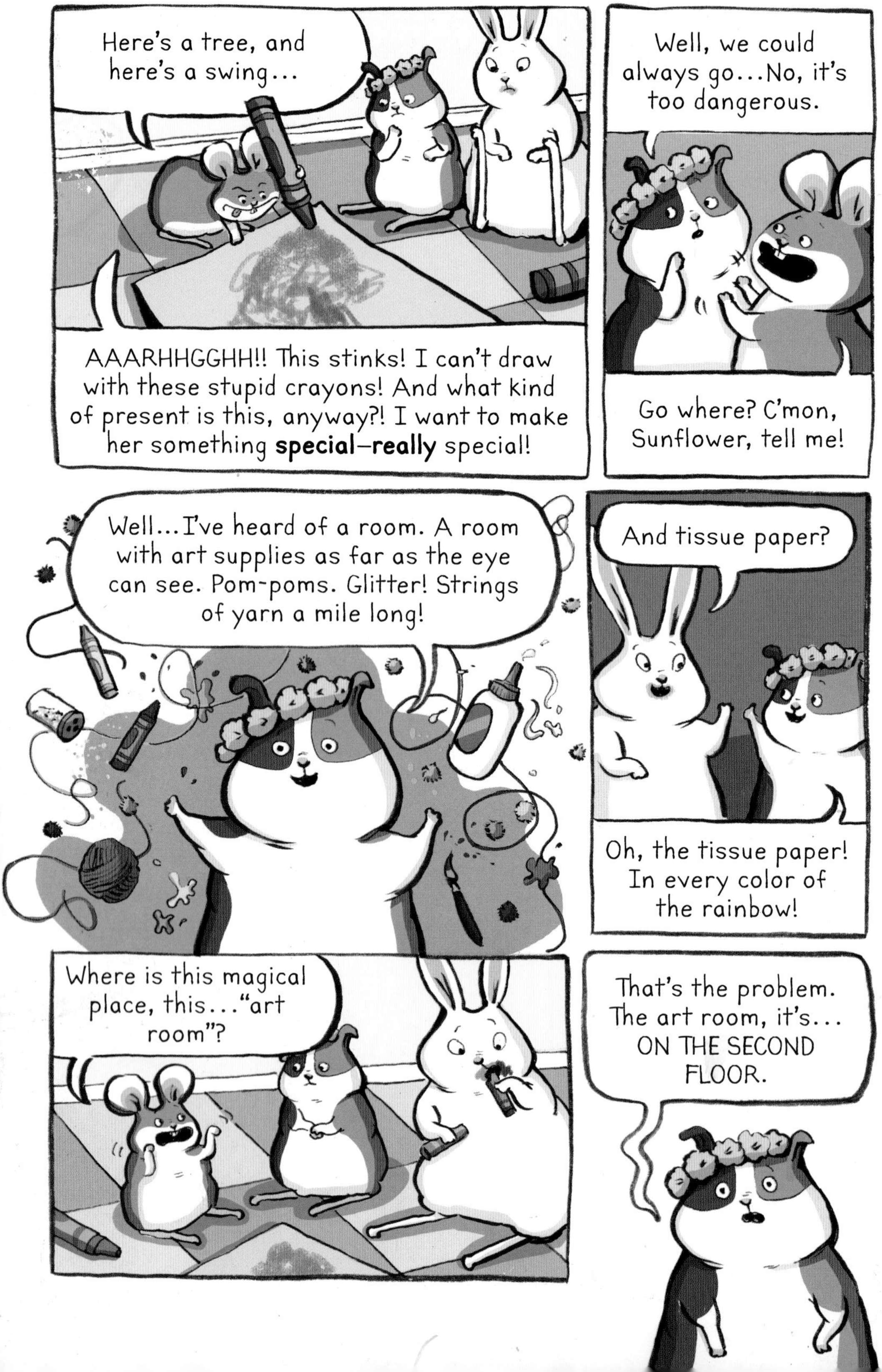
Here's a tree, and here's a swing...
AAARHHGGHH!! This stinks! I can't draw with these stupid crayons! And what kind of present is this, anyway?! I want to make her something **special**—**really** special!
Well, we could always go...No, it's too dangerous.
Go where? C'mon, Sunflower, tell me!
Well...I've heard of a room. A room with art supplies as far as the eye can see. Pom-poms. Glitter! Strings of yarn a mile long!
And tissue paper?
Oh, the tissue paper! In every color of the rainbow!
Where is this magical place, this..."art room"?
That's the problem. The art room, it's... ON THE SECOND FLOOR.

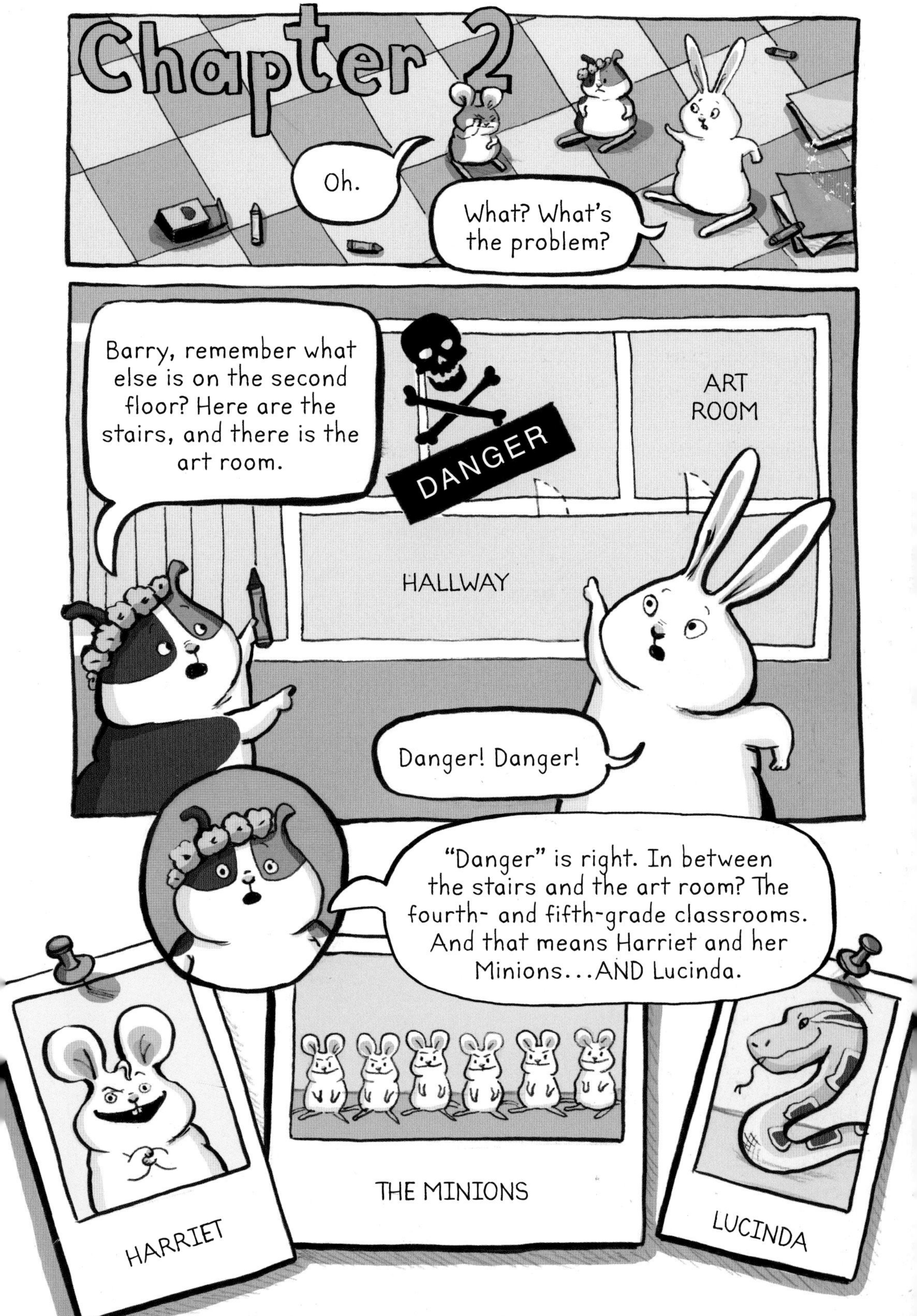

Chapter 2
Oh.
What? What's the problem?
Barry, remember what else is on the second floor? Here are the stairs, and there is the art room.
DANGER
ART ROOM
HALLWAY
Danger! Danger!
"Danger" is right. In between the stairs and the art room? The fourth- and fifth-grade classrooms. And that means Harriet and her Minions...AND Lucinda.
HARRIET
THE MINIONS
LUCINDA

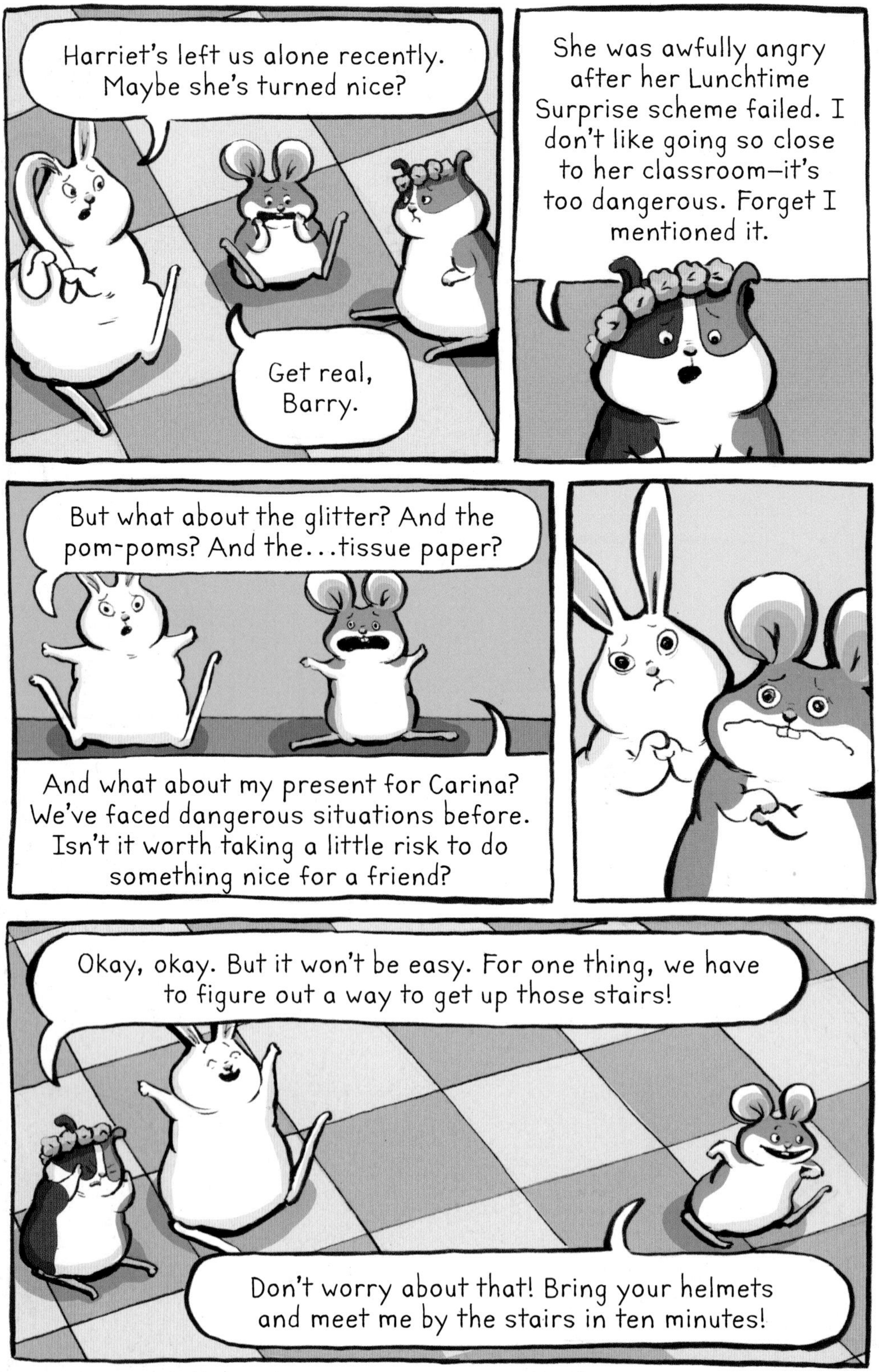
Harriet's left us alone recently. Maybe she's turned nice?
Get real, Barry.
She was awfully angry after her Lunchtime Surprise scheme failed. I don't like going so close to her classroom—it's too dangerous. Forget I mentioned it.
But what about the glitter? And the pom-poms? And the...tissue paper?
And what about my present for Carina? We've faced dangerous situations before. Isn't it worth taking a little risk to do something nice for a friend?
Okay, okay. But it won't be easy. For one thing, we have to figure out a way to get up those stairs!
Don't worry about that! Bring your helmets and meet me by the stairs in ten minutes!

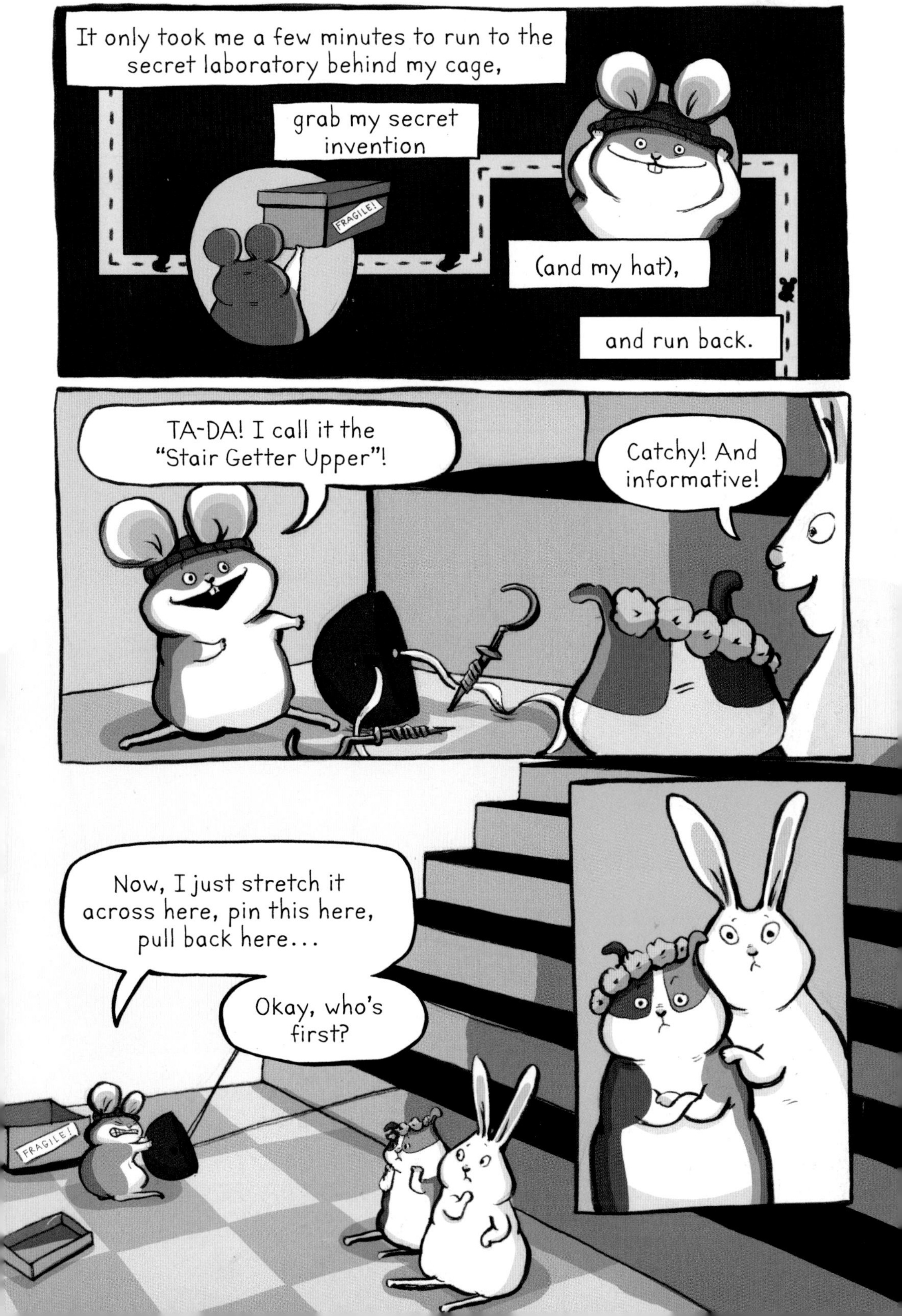

It only took me a few minutes to run to the secret laboratory behind my cage,
grab my secret invention
FRAGILE!
(and my hat),
and run back.
TA-DA! I call it the "Stair Getter Upper"!
Catchy! And informative!
Now, I just stretch it across here, pin this here, pull back here...
Okay, who's first?
FRAGILE!

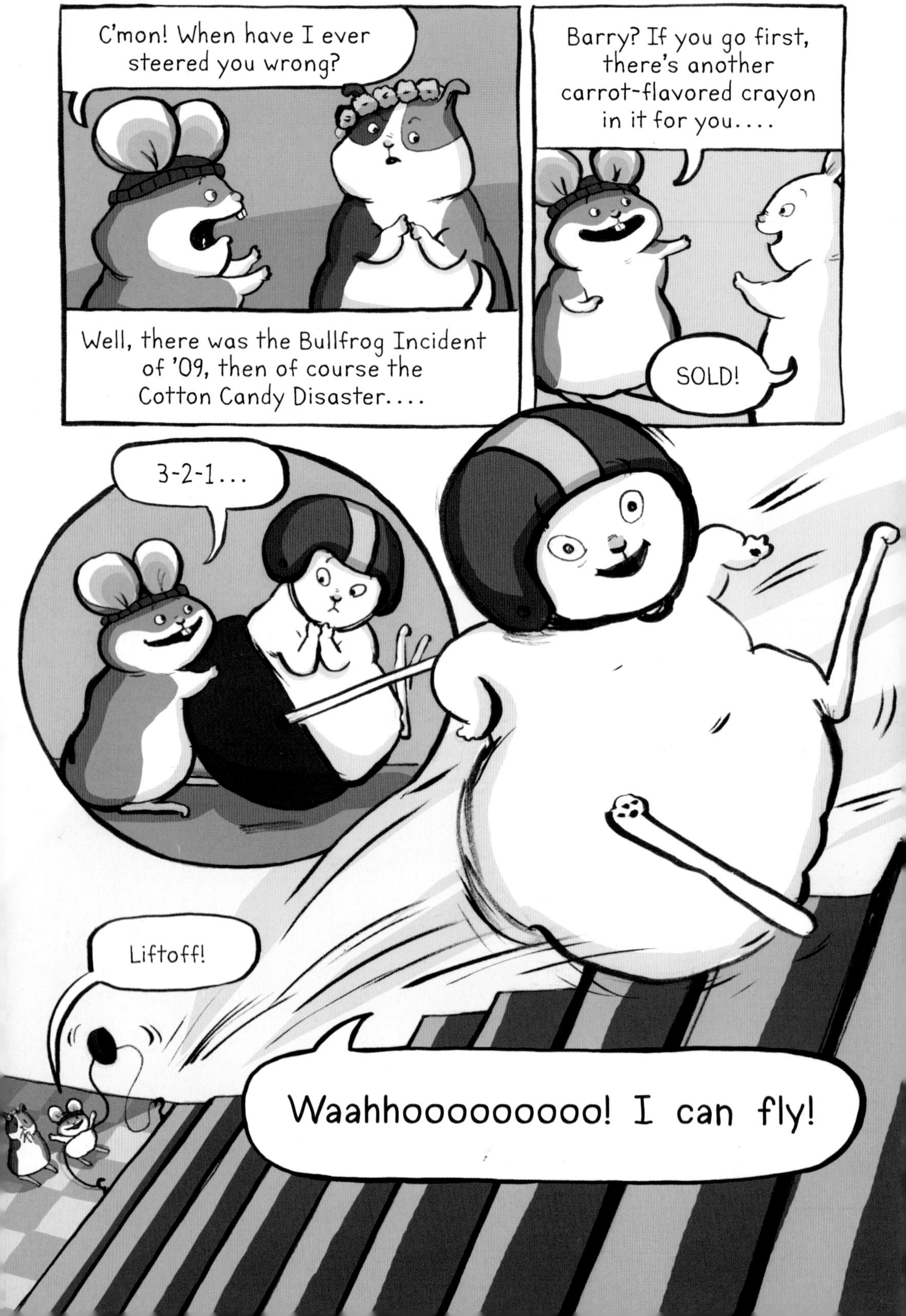
C'mon! When have I ever steered you wrong?
Well, there was the Bullfrog Incident of '09, then of course the Cotton Candy Disaster....
Barry? If you go first, there's another carrot-flavored crayon in it for you....
SOLD!
3-2-1...
Liftoff!
Waahhoooooooooo! I can fly!

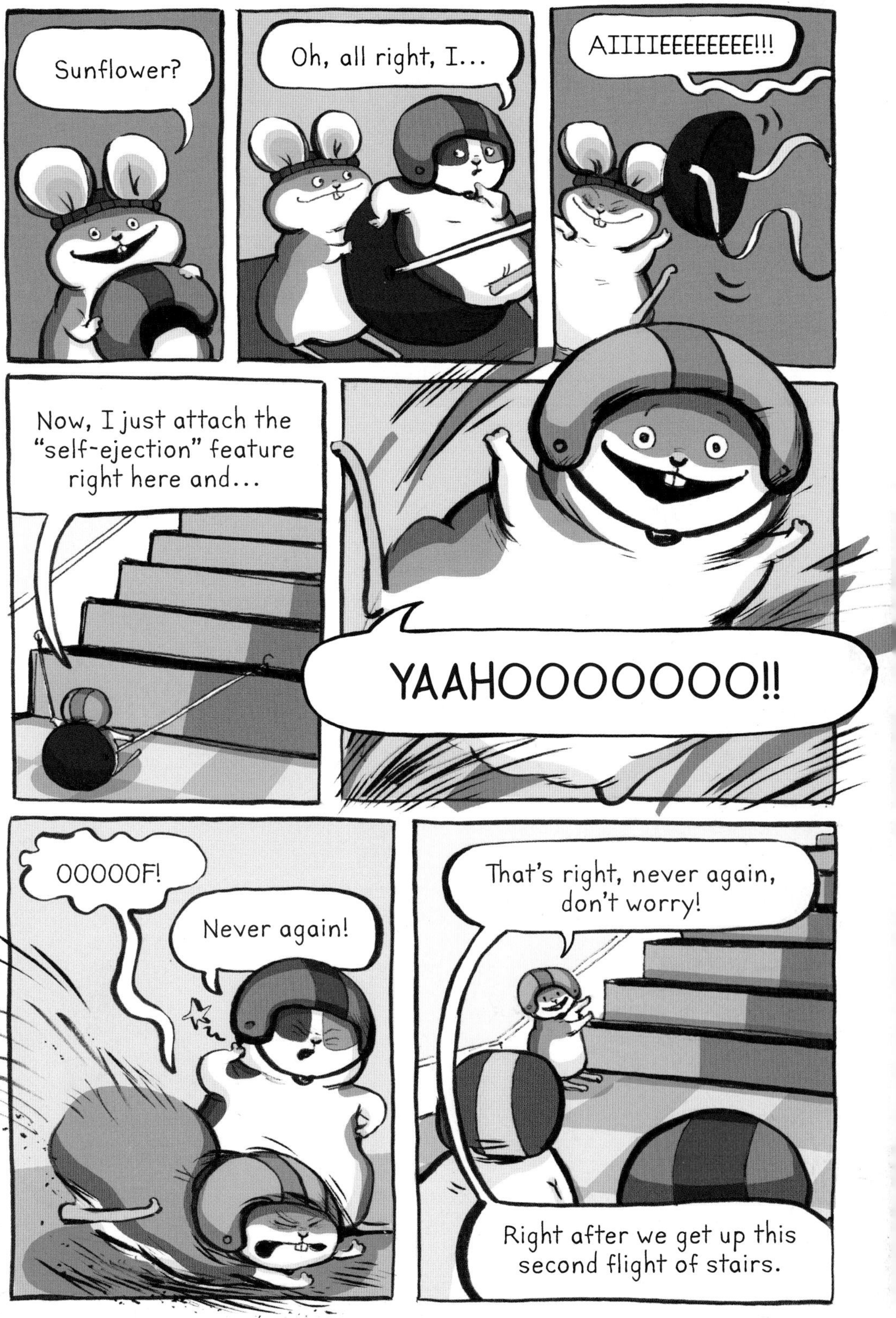
Sunflower?
Oh, all right, I...
AIIIIEEEEEEEEE!!!
Now, I just attach the "self-ejection" feature right here and...
YAAHOOOOOOOO!!
OOOOOF!
Never again!
That's right, never again, don't worry!
Right after we get up this second flight of stairs.

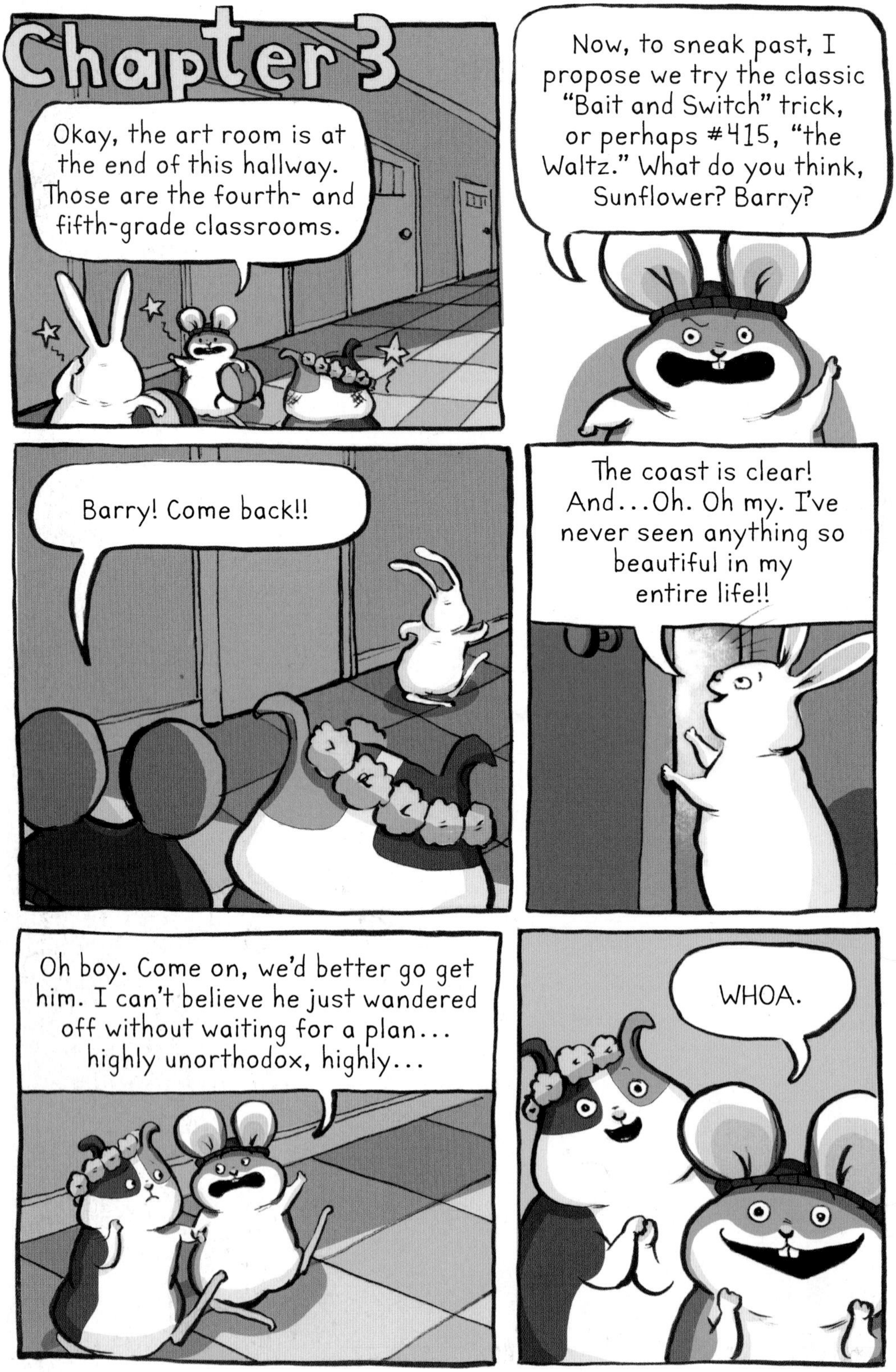
Chapter 3
Okay, the art room is at the end of this hallway. Those are the fourth- and fifth-grade classrooms.
Now, to sneak past, I propose we try the classic "Bait and Switch" trick, or perhaps #415, "the Waltz." What do you think, Sunflower? Barry?
Barry! Come back!!
The coast is clear! And...Oh. Oh my. I've never seen anything so beautiful in my entire life!!
Oh boy. Come on, we'd better go get him. I can't believe he just wandered off without waiting for a plan... highly unorthodox, highly...
WHOA.

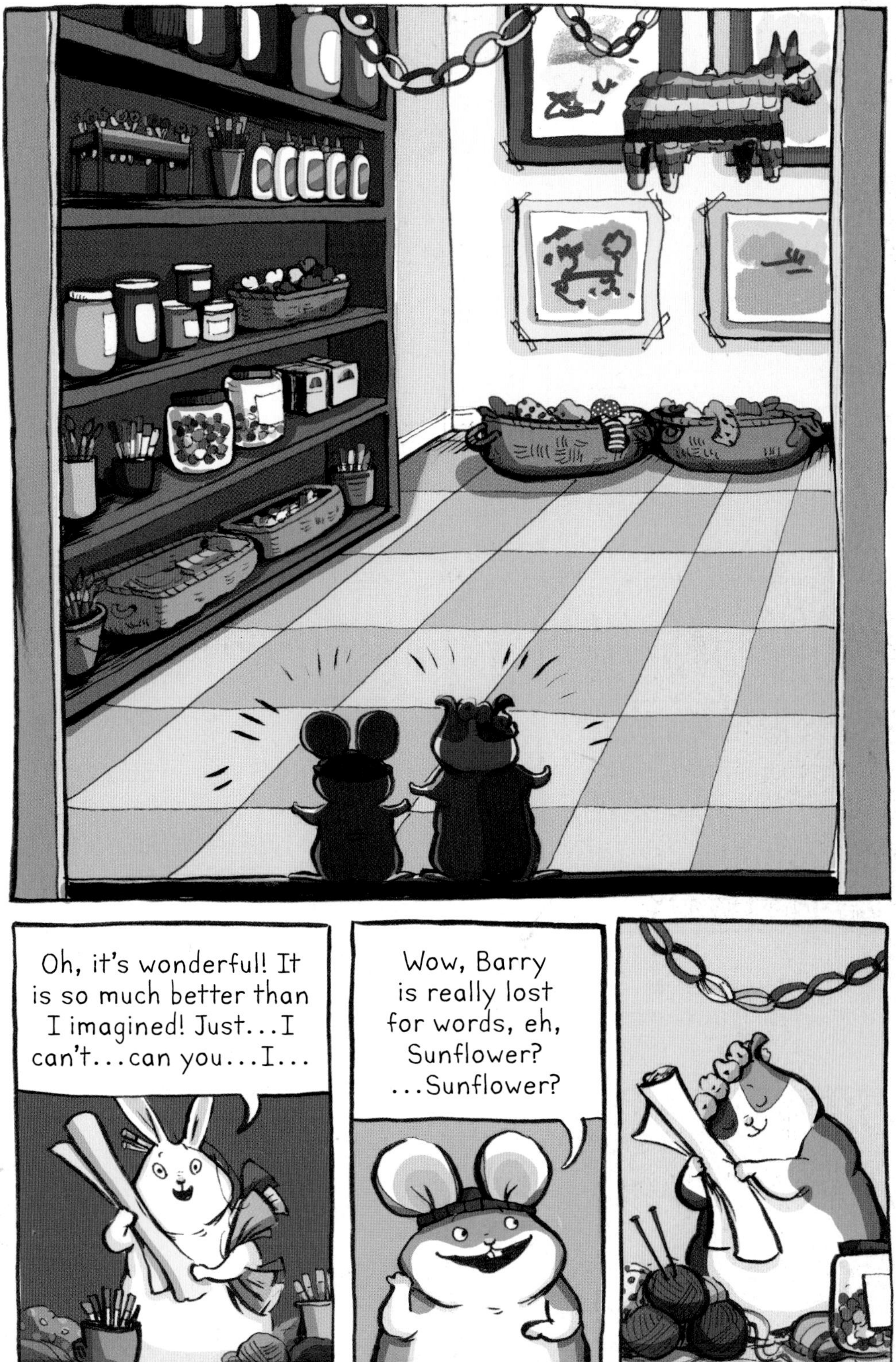
Oh, it's wonderful! It is so much better than I imagined! Just...I can't...can you...I...
Wow, Barry is really lost for words, eh, Sunflower? ...Sunflower?

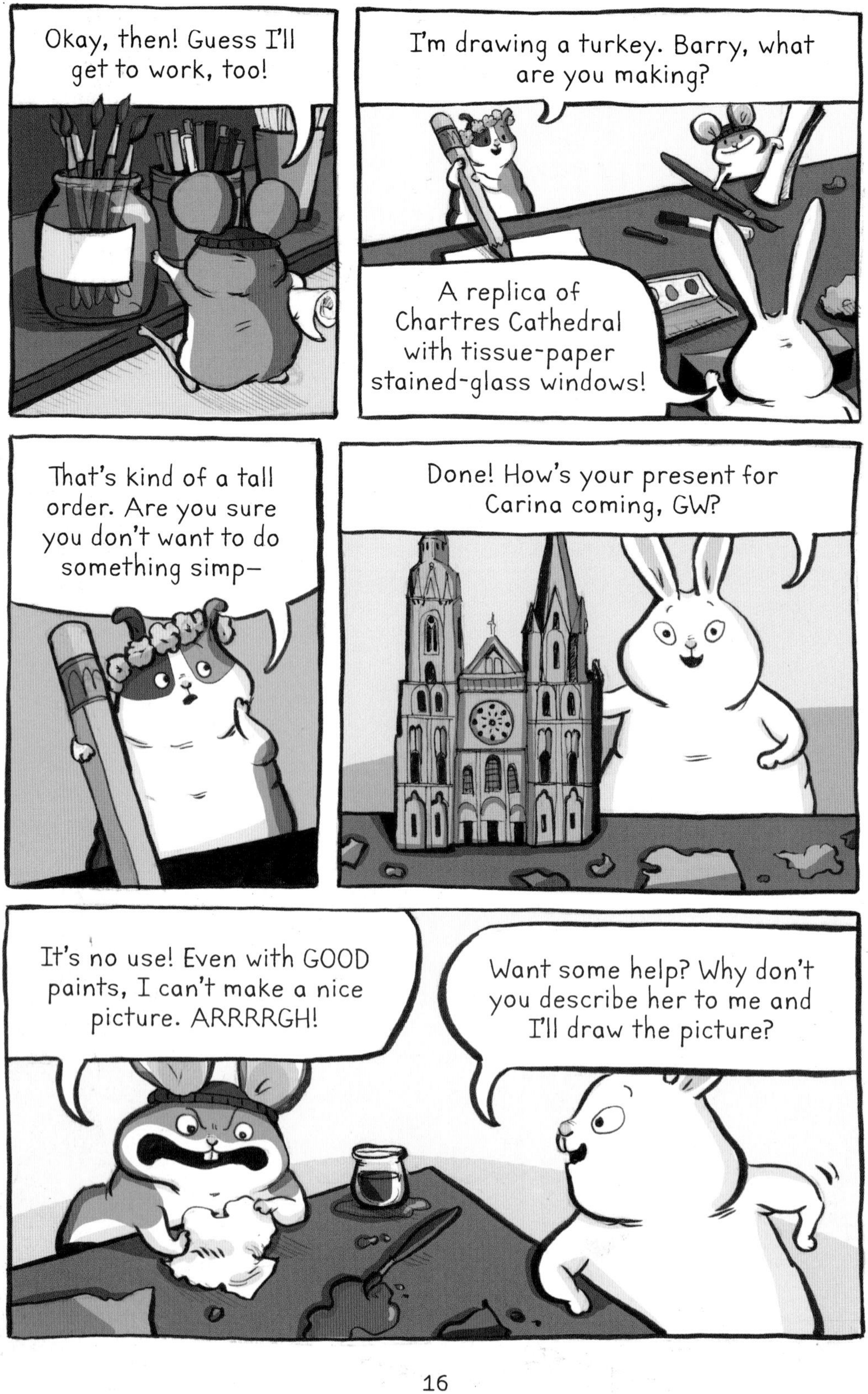
Okay, then! Guess I'll get to work, too!
I'm drawing a turkey. Barry, what are you making?
A replica of Chartres Cathedral with tissue-paper stained-glass windows!
That's kind of a tall order. Are you sure you don't want to do something simp–
Done! How's your present for Carina coming, GW?
It's no use! Even with GOOD paints, I can't make a nice picture. ARRRRGH!
Want some help? Why don't you describe her to me and I'll draw the picture?

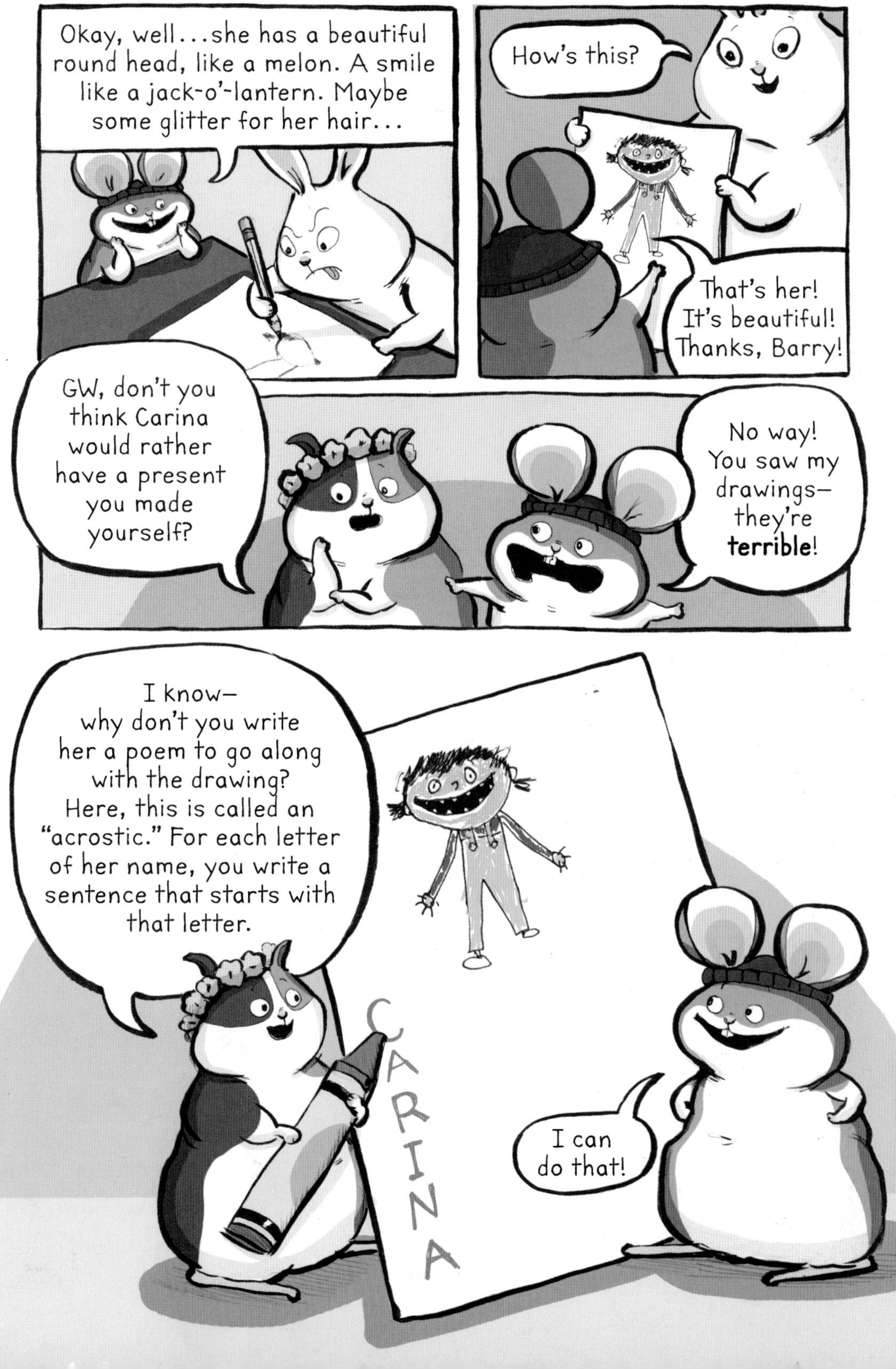

Okay, well...she has a beautiful round head, like a melon. A smile like a jack-o'-lantern. Maybe some glitter for her hair...
How's this?
That's her! It's beautiful! Thanks, Barry!
GW, don't you think Carina would rather have a present you made yourself?
No way! You saw my drawings—they're **terrible**!
I know—why don't you write her a poem to go along with the drawing? Here, this is called an "acrostic." For each letter of her name, you write a sentence that starts with that letter.
CARINA
I can do that!

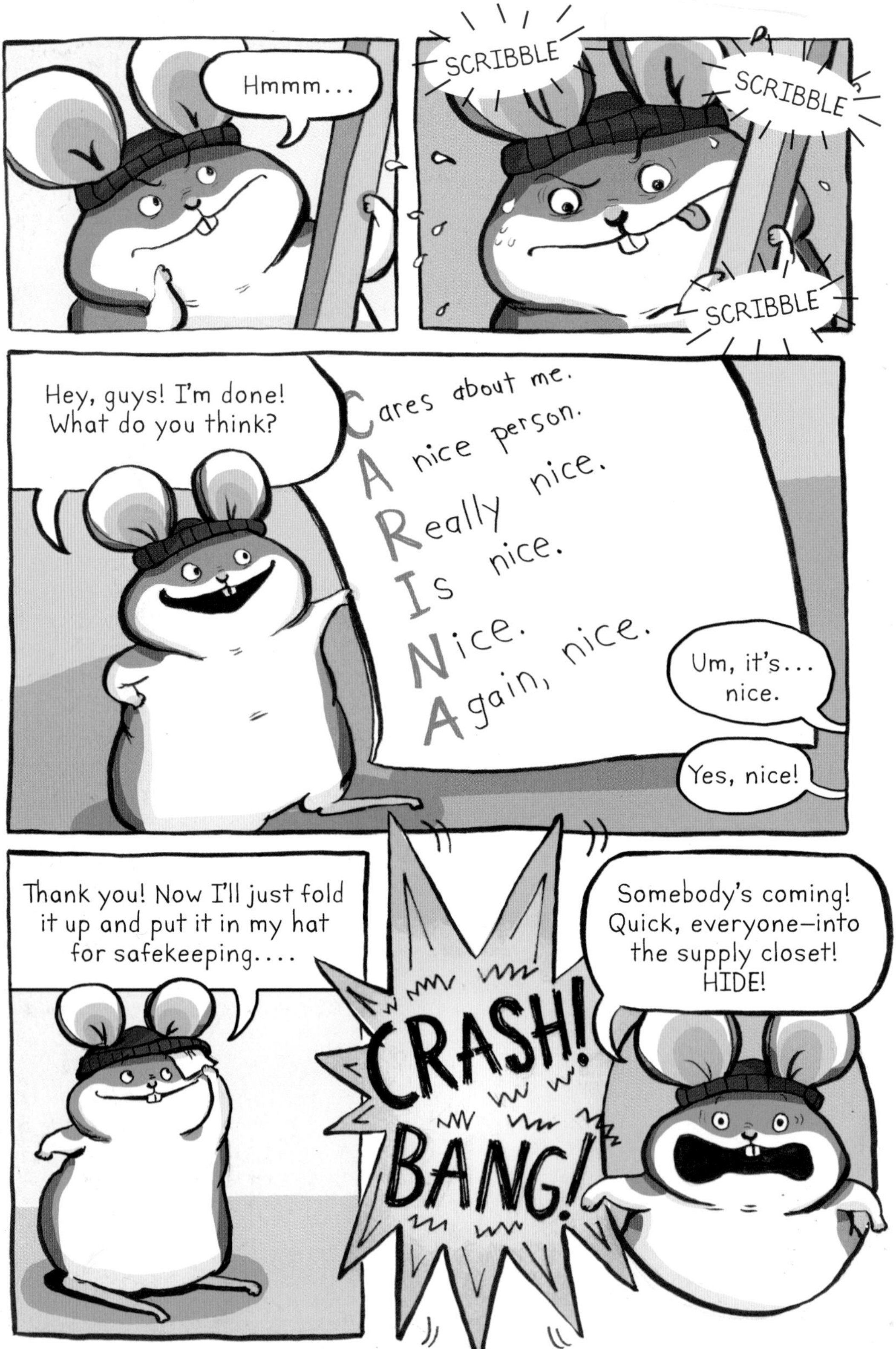
Hmmm...
SCRIBBLE
SCRIBBLE
SCRIBBLE
Hey, guys! I'm done! What do you think?
Cares about me.
A nice person.
Really nice.
Is nice.
Nice.
Again, nice.
Um, it's... nice.
Yes, nice!
Thank you! Now I'll just fold it up and put it in my hat for safekeeping....
CRASH!
BANG!
Somebody's coming! Quick, everyone—into the supply closet! HIDE!

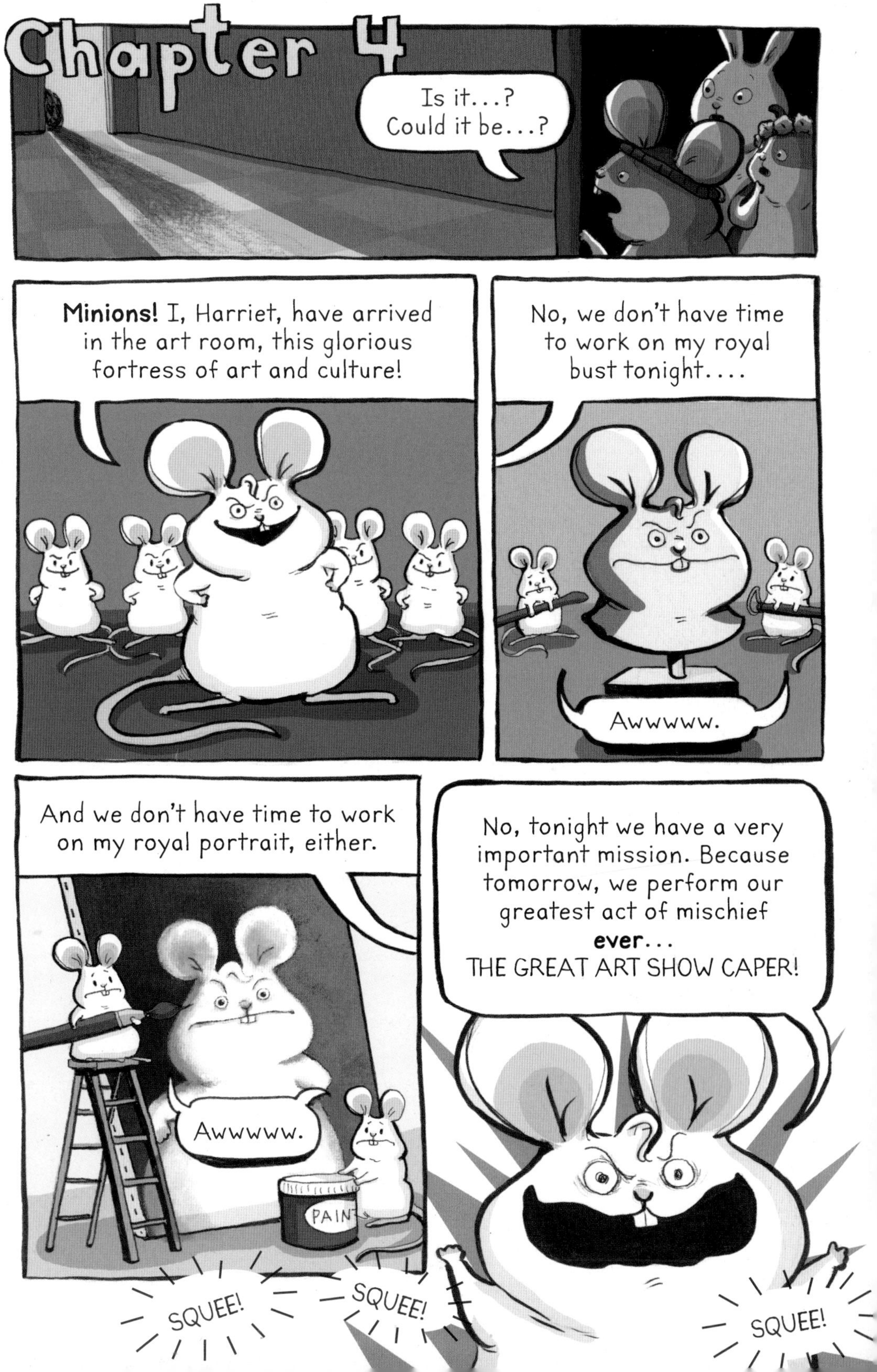
Chapter 4
Is it...? Could it be...?
Minions! I, Harriet, have arrived in the art room, this glorious fortress of art and culture!
No, we don't have time to work on my royal bust tonight....
Awwwww.
And we don't have time to work on my royal portrait, either.
Awwwww.
PAINT
No, tonight we have a very important mission. Because tomorrow, we perform our greatest act of mischief **ever**... THE GREAT ART SHOW CAPER!
SQUEE!
SQUEE!
SQUEE!

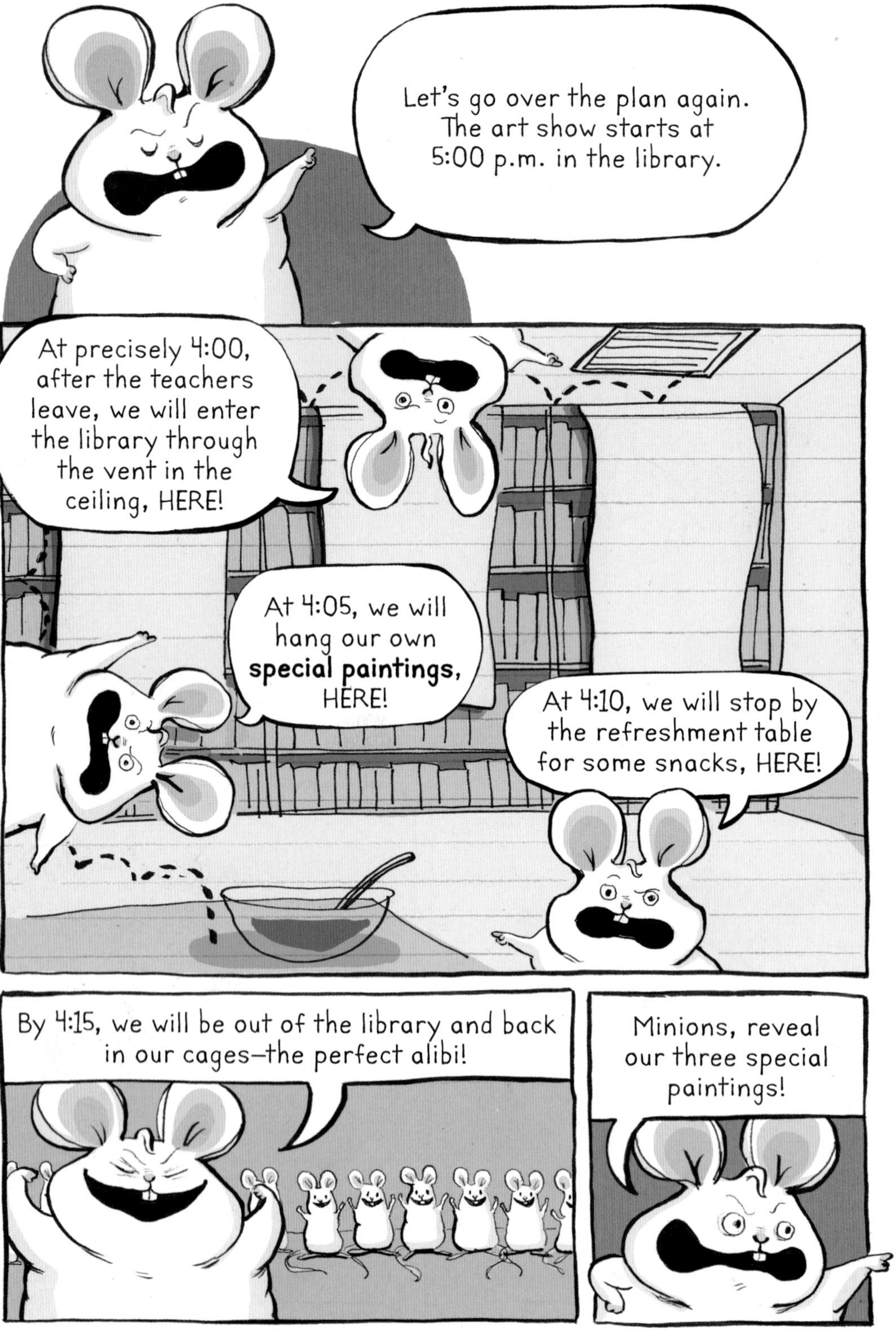
Let's go over the plan again. The art show starts at 5:00 p.m. in the library.
At precisely 4:00, after the teachers leave, we will enter the library through the vent in the ceiling, HERE!
At 4:05, we will hang our own **special paintings,** HERE!
At 4:10, we will stop by the refreshment table for some snacks, HERE!
By 4:15, we will be out of the library and back in our cages—the perfect alibi!
Minions, reveal our three special paintings!

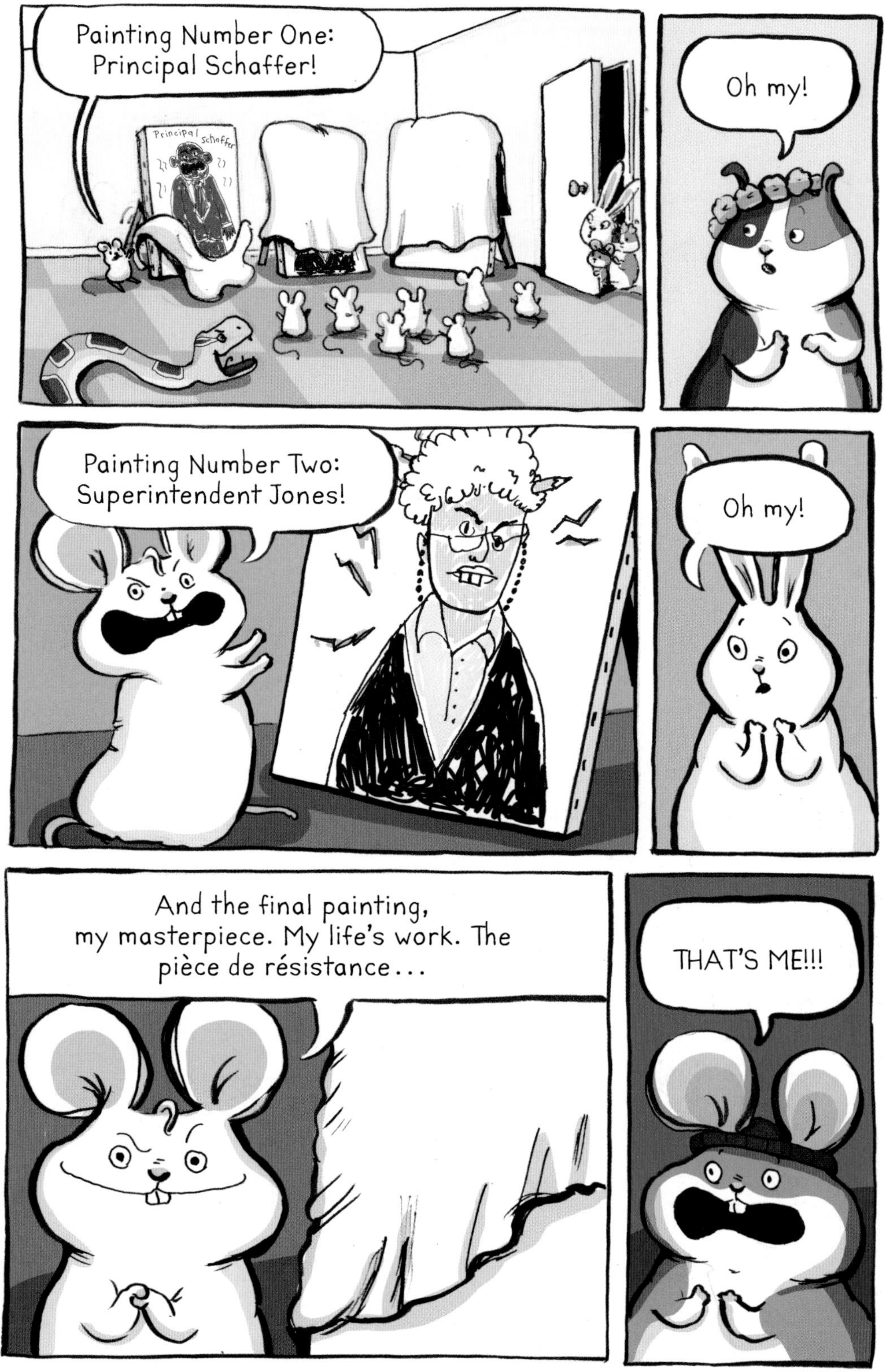
Painting Number One:
Principal Schaffer!
Principal Schaffer
Oh my!
Painting Number Two:
Superintendent Jones!
Oh my!
And the final painting,
my masterpiece. My life's work. The
pièce de résistance...
THAT'S ME!!!

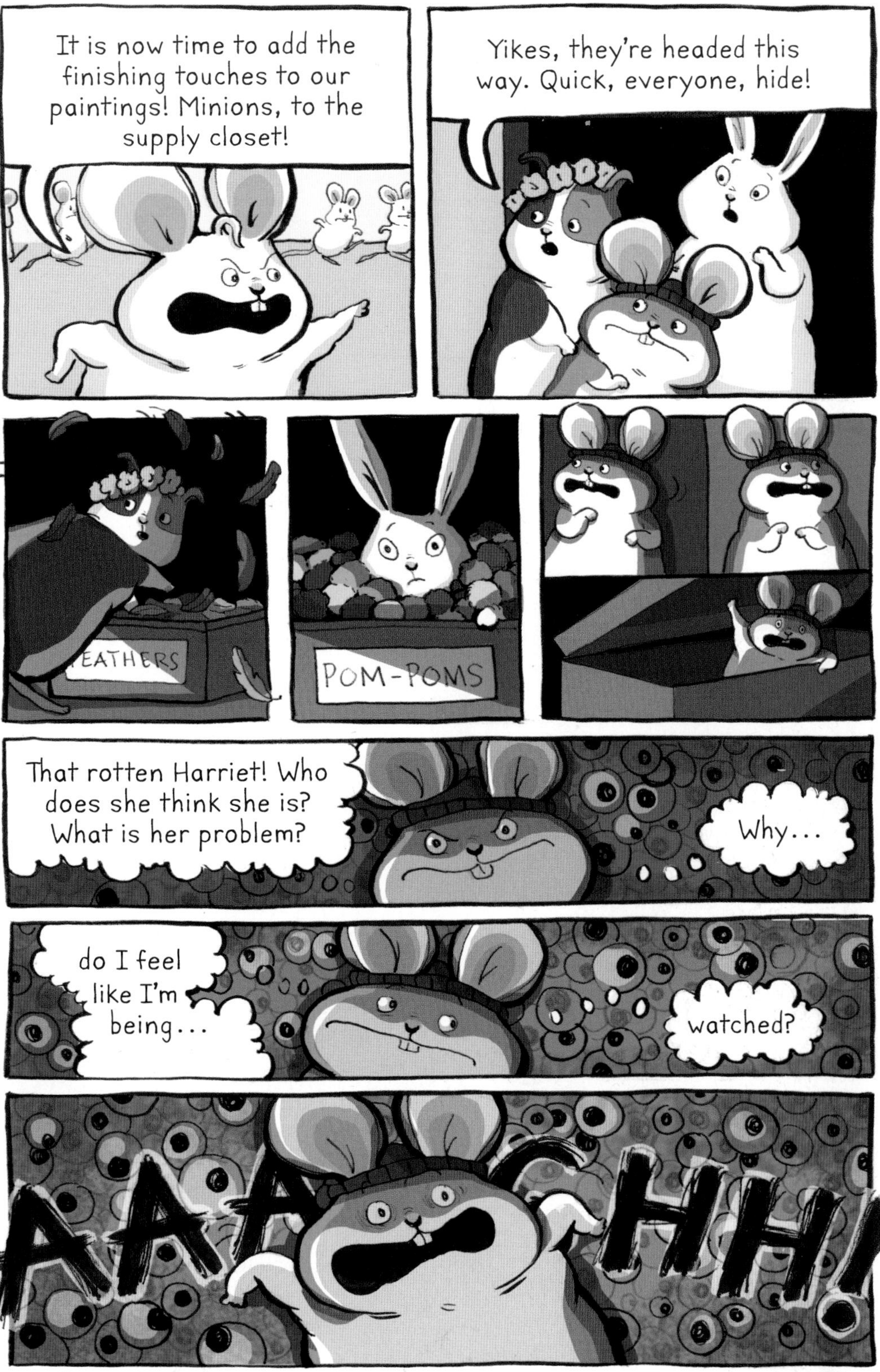
It is now time to add the finishing touches to our paintings! Minions, to the supply closet!
Yikes, they're headed this way. Quick, everyone, hide!
FEATHERS
POM-POMS
That rotten Harriet! Who does she think she is? What is her problem?
Why...
do I feel like I'm being...
watched?
AAAHHH!

AAAGGGHHH!!

GOOGLY EYES

Huh?

R-R-R-RIP!

Oh-ho, what do we have here?! Minions, look around—those two other furballs must be nearby!

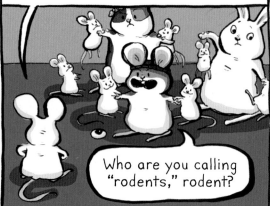

You just can't stay away from trouble, can you, rodents?

Who are you calling "rodents," rodent?

Tough guy, eh? You won't be so tough when you're sent to St. Bart's Obedience School for Unruly Pets! Here, take a brochure!

ST. BART'S
Obedience School
for Unruly Pets

Oooh, they have an exercise room!

Minions, tie these animals up!

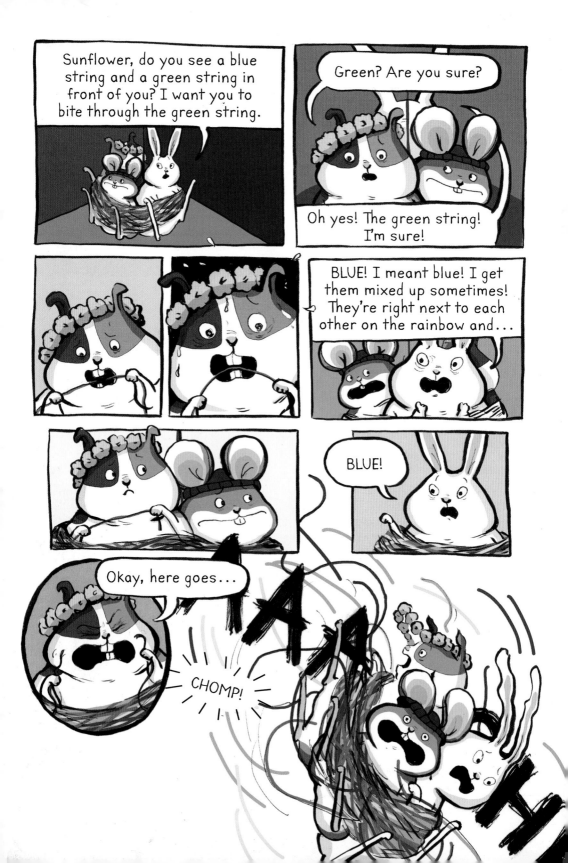

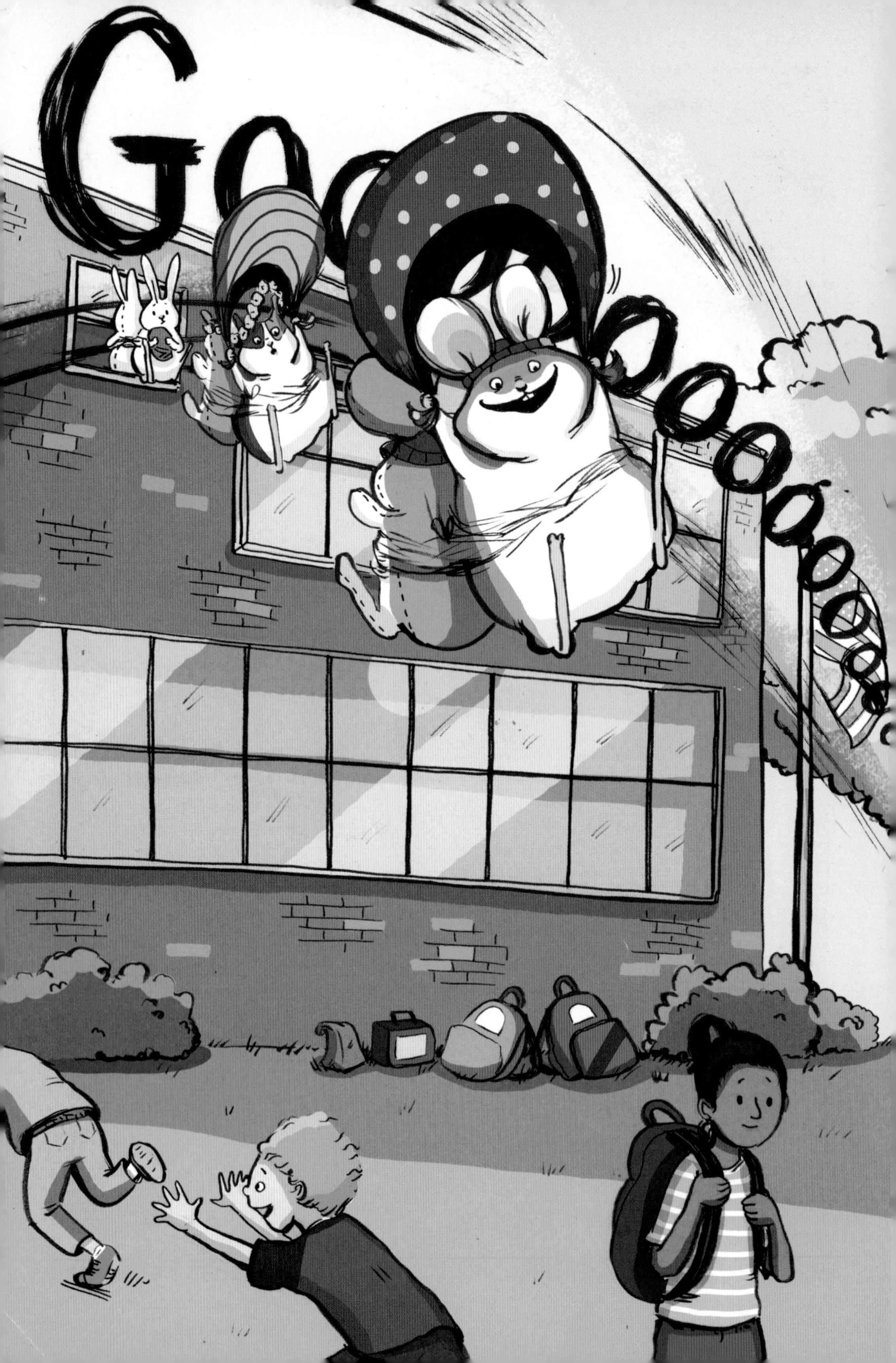
Goooooooooo

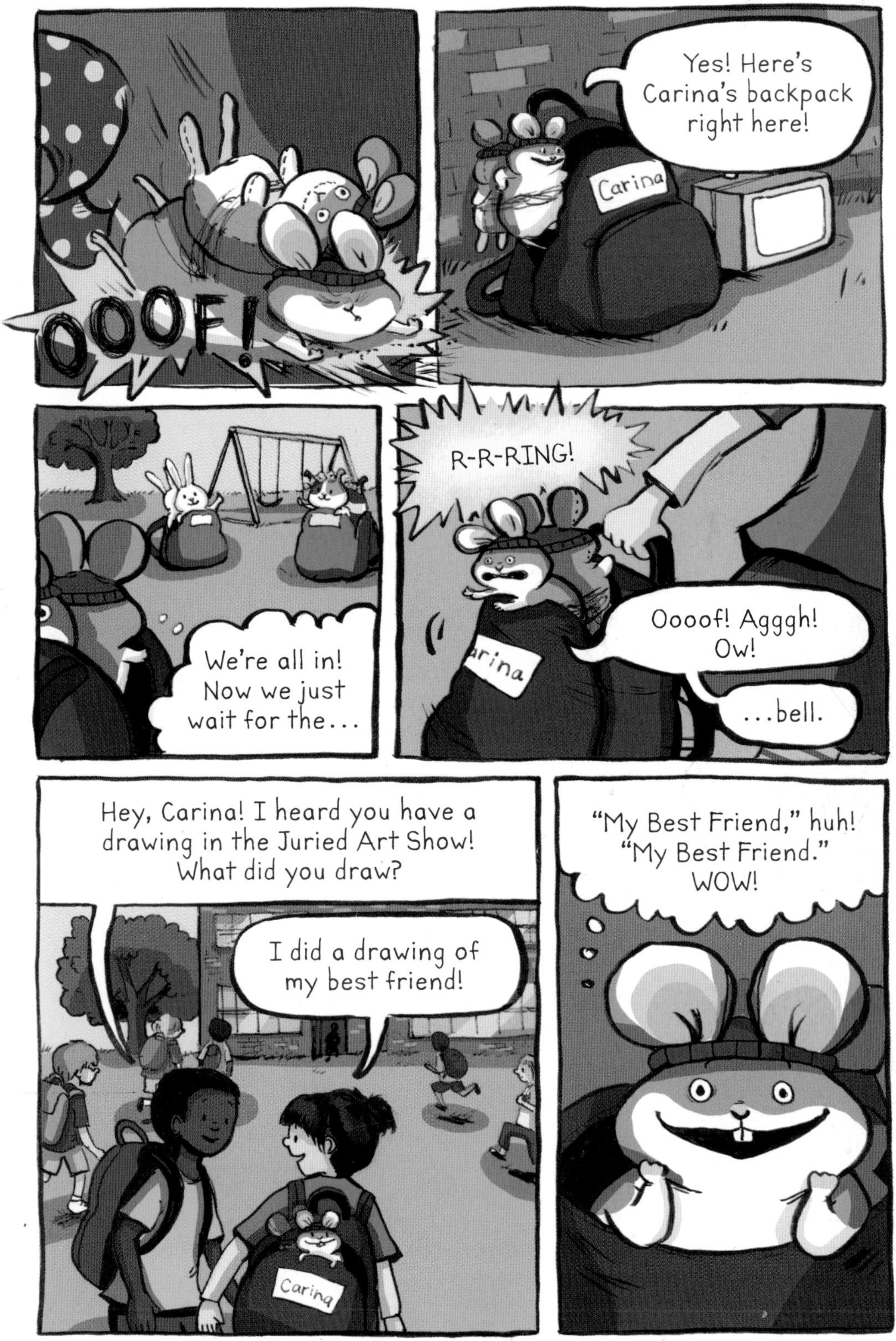
OOOF!
Yes! Here's Carina's backpack right here!
Carina
We're all in! Now we just wait for the...
R-R-RING!
Oooof! Agggh! Ow!
...bell.
arina
Hey, Carina! I heard you have a drawing in the Juried Art Show! What did you draw?
I did a drawing of my best friend!
Carina
"My Best Friend," huh! "My Best Friend." WOW!

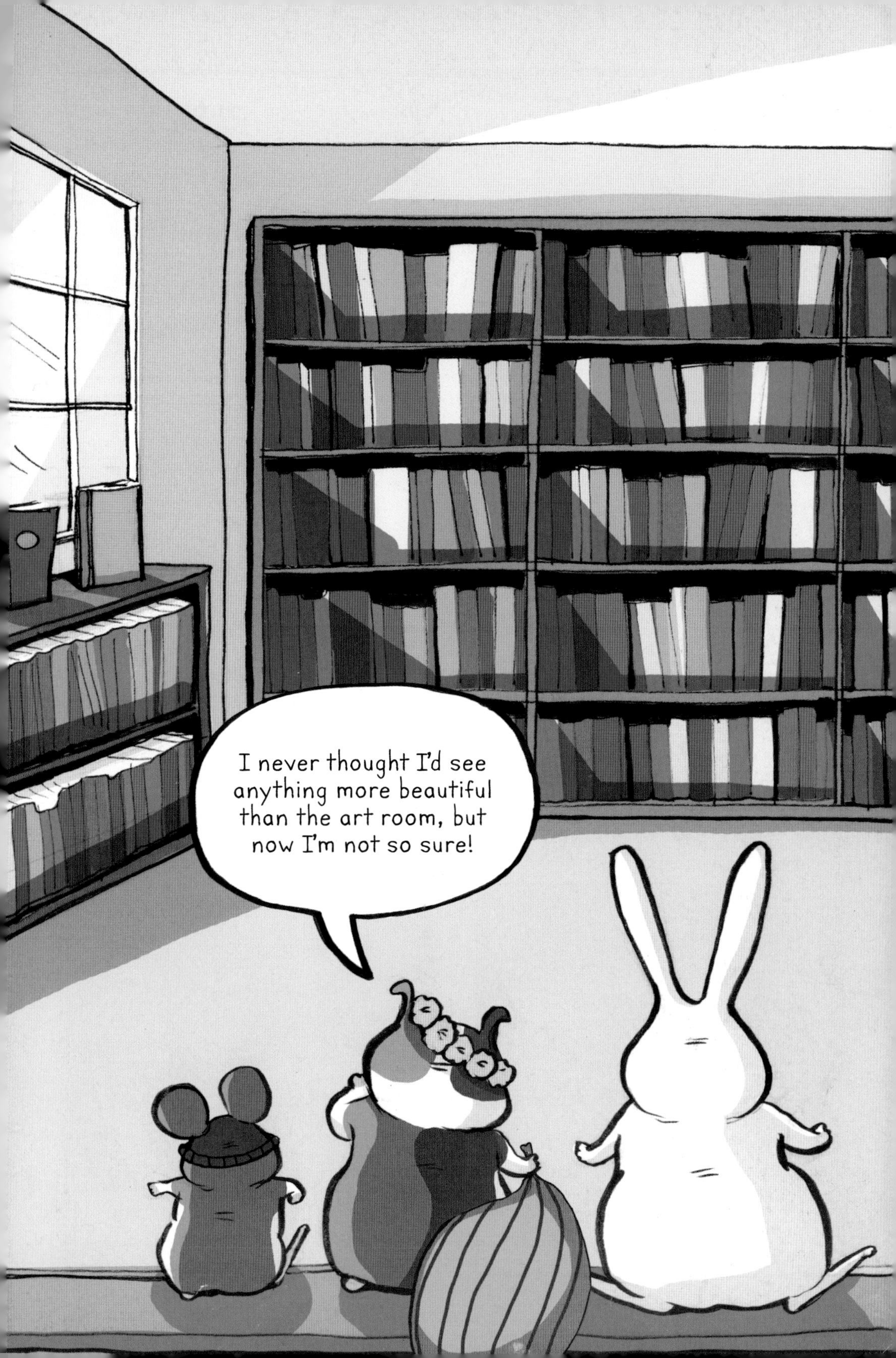
I never thought I'd see anything more beautiful than the art room, but now I'm not so sure!

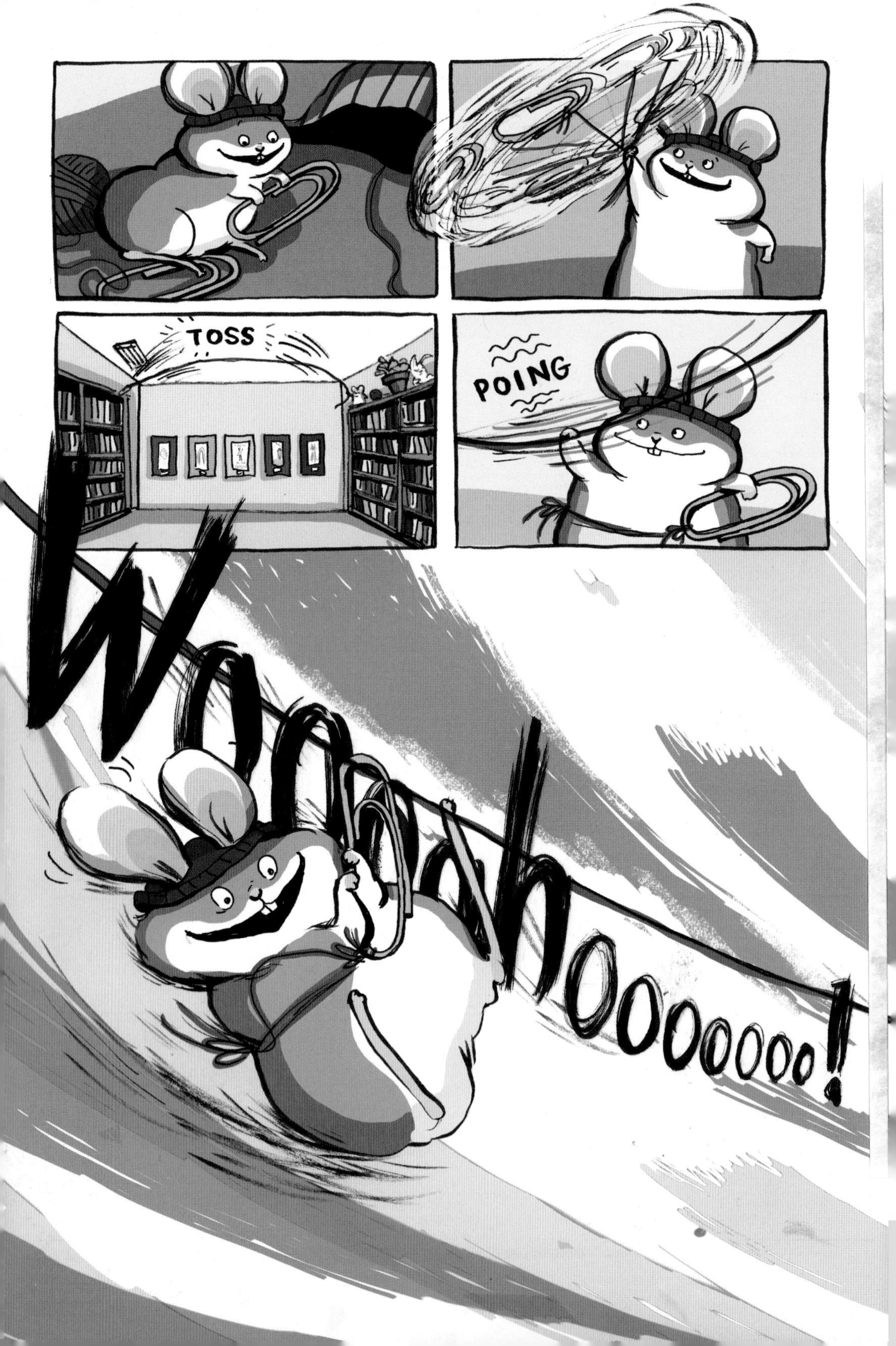
TOSS
POING
Wooooahoooooooo!

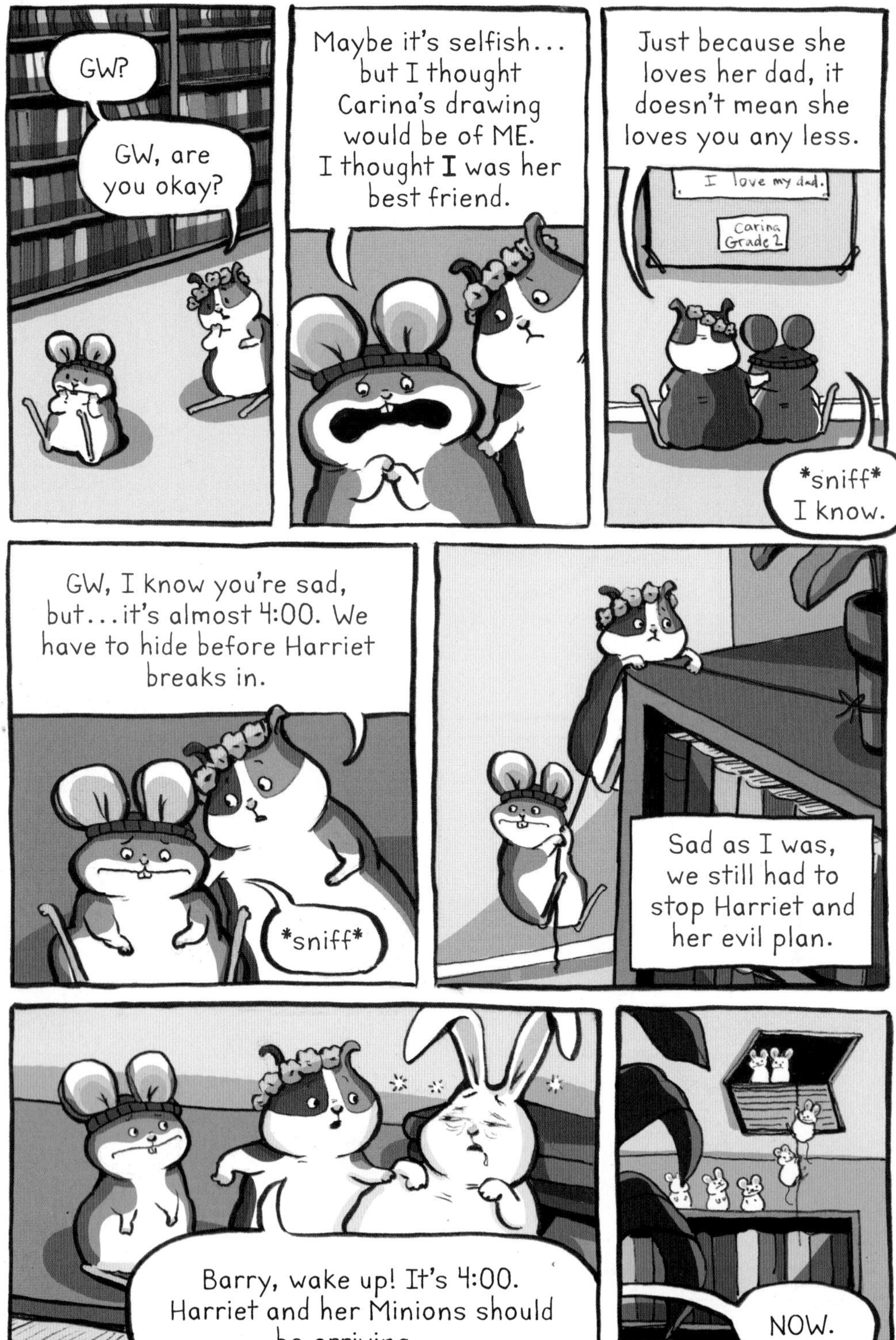
GW?
GW, are you okay?
Maybe it's selfish... but I thought Carina's drawing would be of ME. I thought I was her best friend.
Just because she loves her dad, it doesn't mean she loves you any less.
I love my dad.
Carina Grade 2
sniff I know.
GW, I know you're sad, but...it's almost 4:00. We have to hide before Harriet breaks in.
sniff
Sad as I was, we still had to stop Harriet and her evil plan.
Barry, wake up! It's 4:00. Harriet and her Minions should be arriving...
NOW.

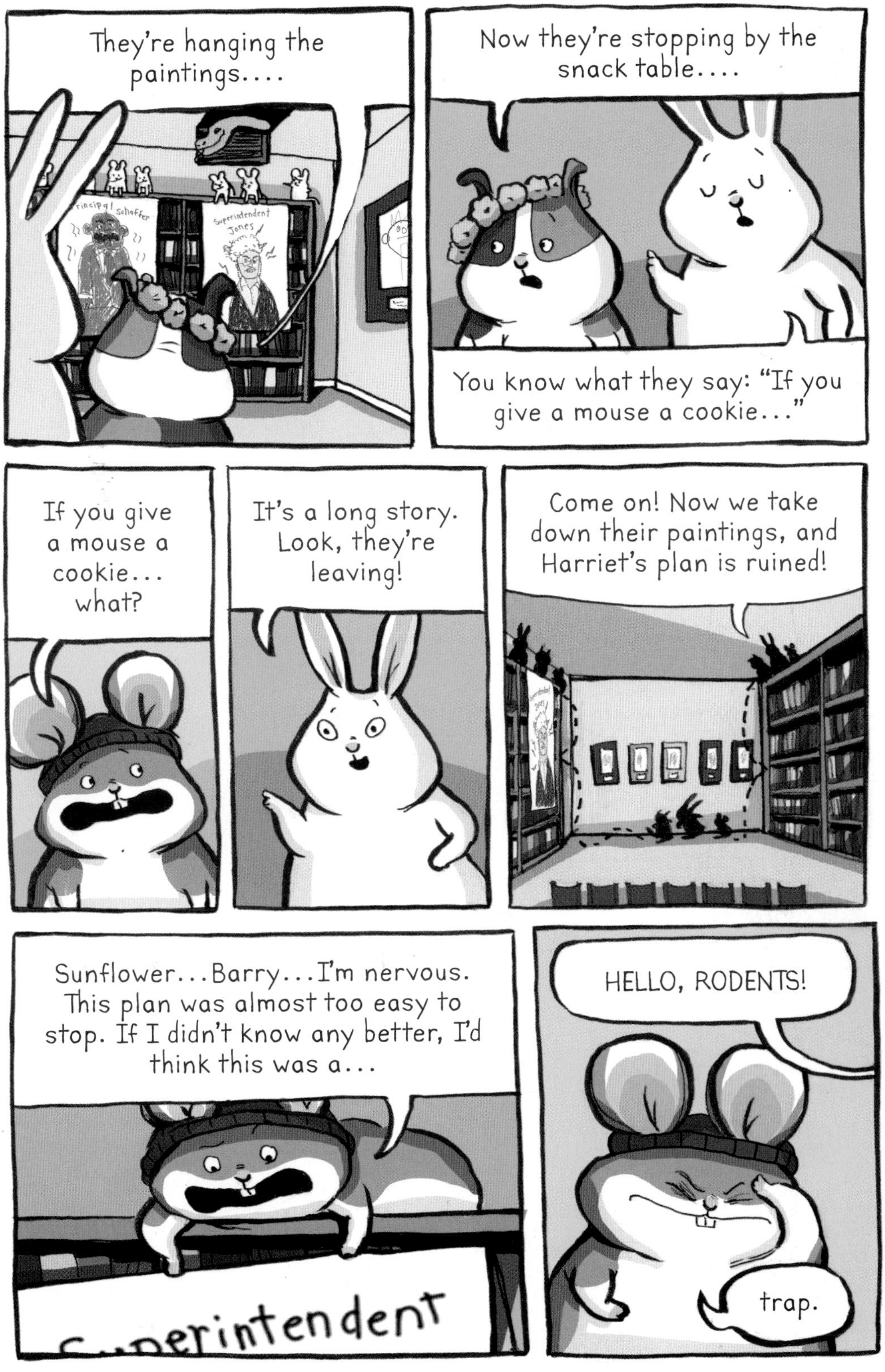
They're hanging the paintings....
Now they're stopping by the snack table....
You know what they say: "If you give a mouse a cookie..."
If you give a mouse a cookie... what?
It's a long story. Look, they're leaving!
Come on! Now we take down their paintings, and Harriet's plan is ruined!
Sunflower...Barry...I'm nervous. This plan was almost too easy to stop. If I didn't know any better, I'd think this was a...
HELLO, RODENTS!
trap.

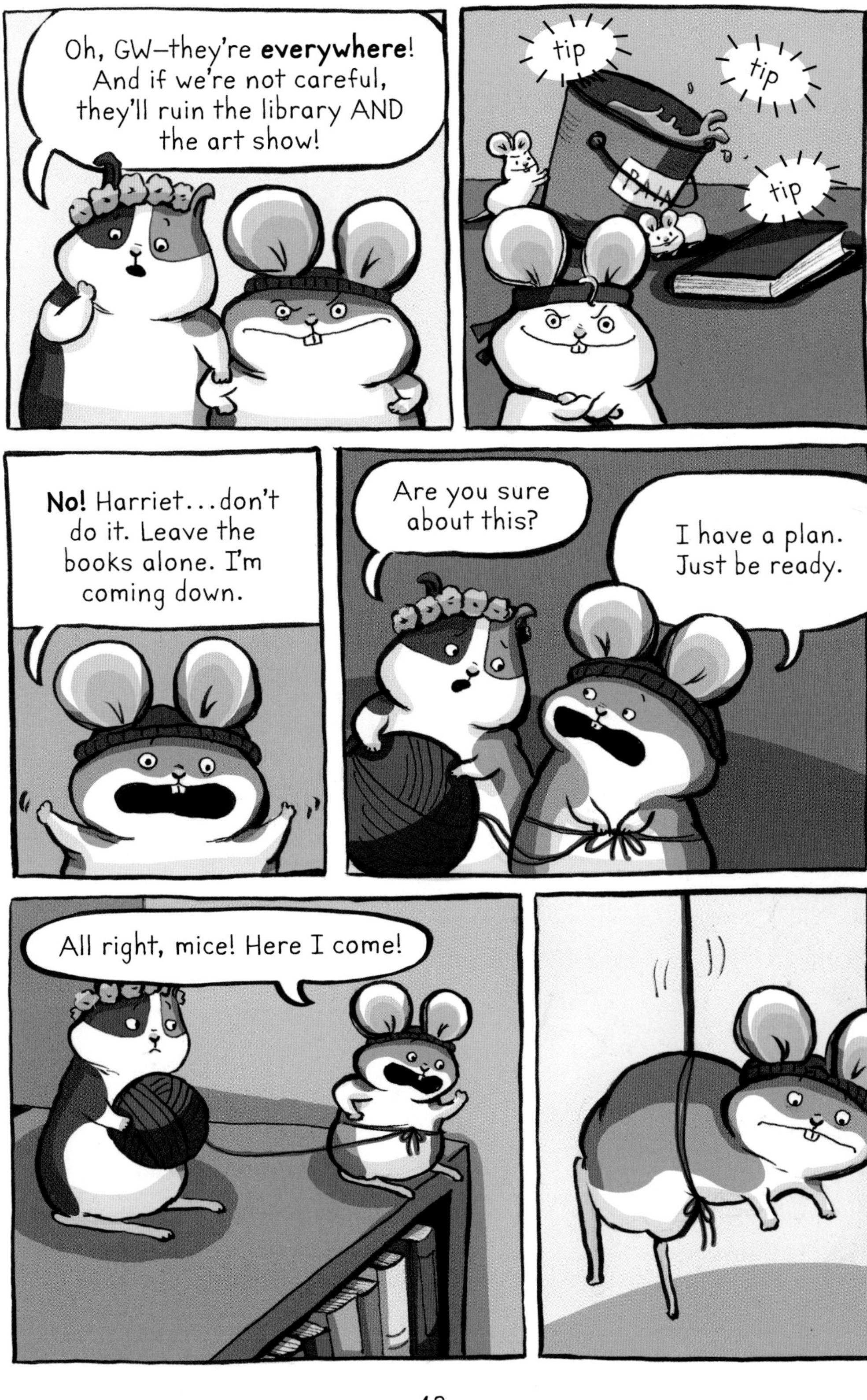

Oh, GW—they're **everywhere**! And if we're not careful, they'll ruin the library AND the art show!
tip
tip
tip
No! Harriet...don't do it. Leave the books alone. I'm coming down.
Are you sure about this?
I have a plan. Just be ready.
All right, mice! Here I come!

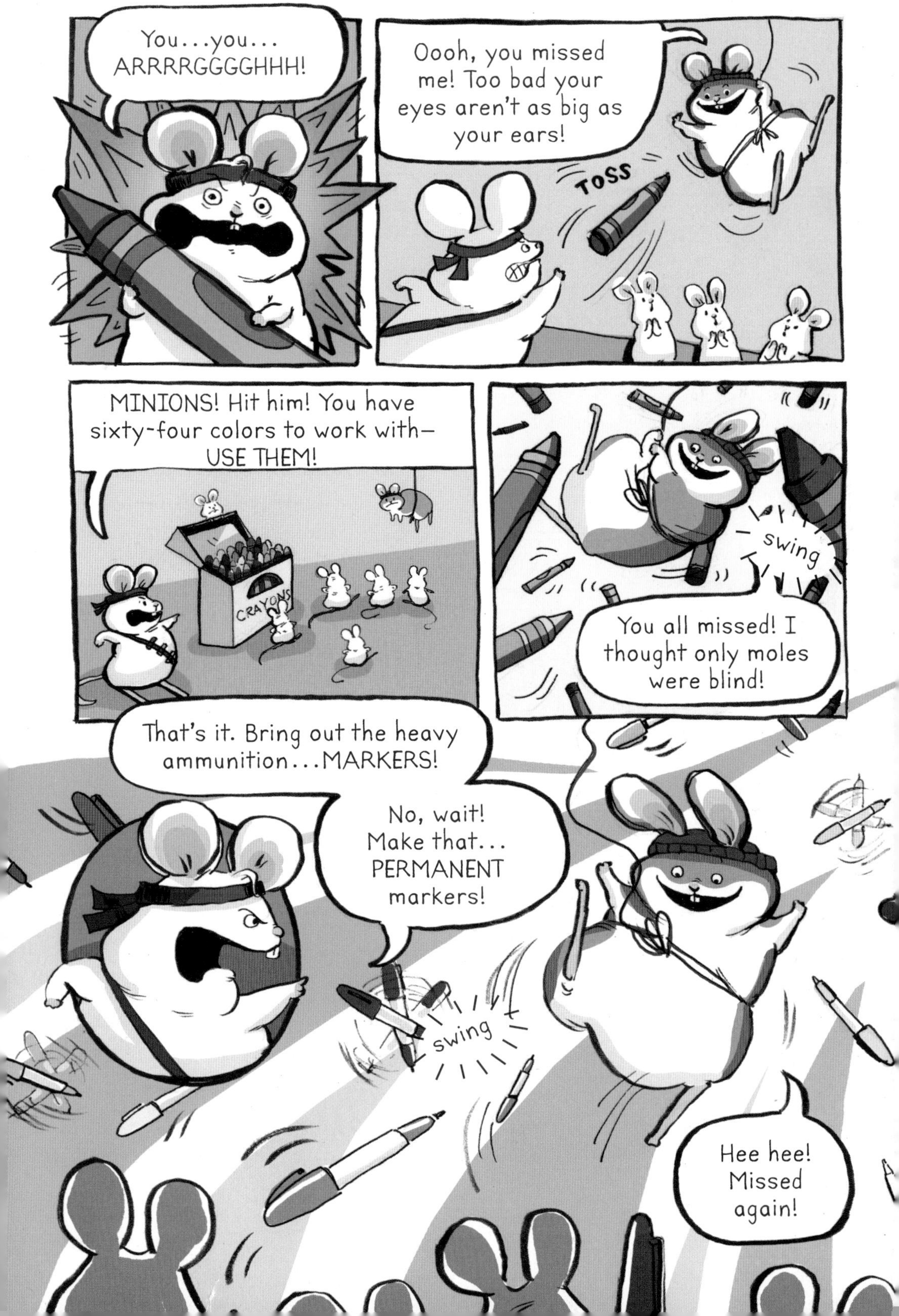
You...you... ARRRRGGGGHHH!
Oooh, you missed me! Too bad your eyes aren't as big as your ears!
TOSS
MINIONS! Hit him! You have sixty-four colors to work with—USE THEM!
CRAYONS
swing
You all missed! I thought only moles were blind!
That's it. Bring out the heavy ammunition...MARKERS!
No, wait! Make that... PERMANENT markers!
swing
Hee hee! Missed again!

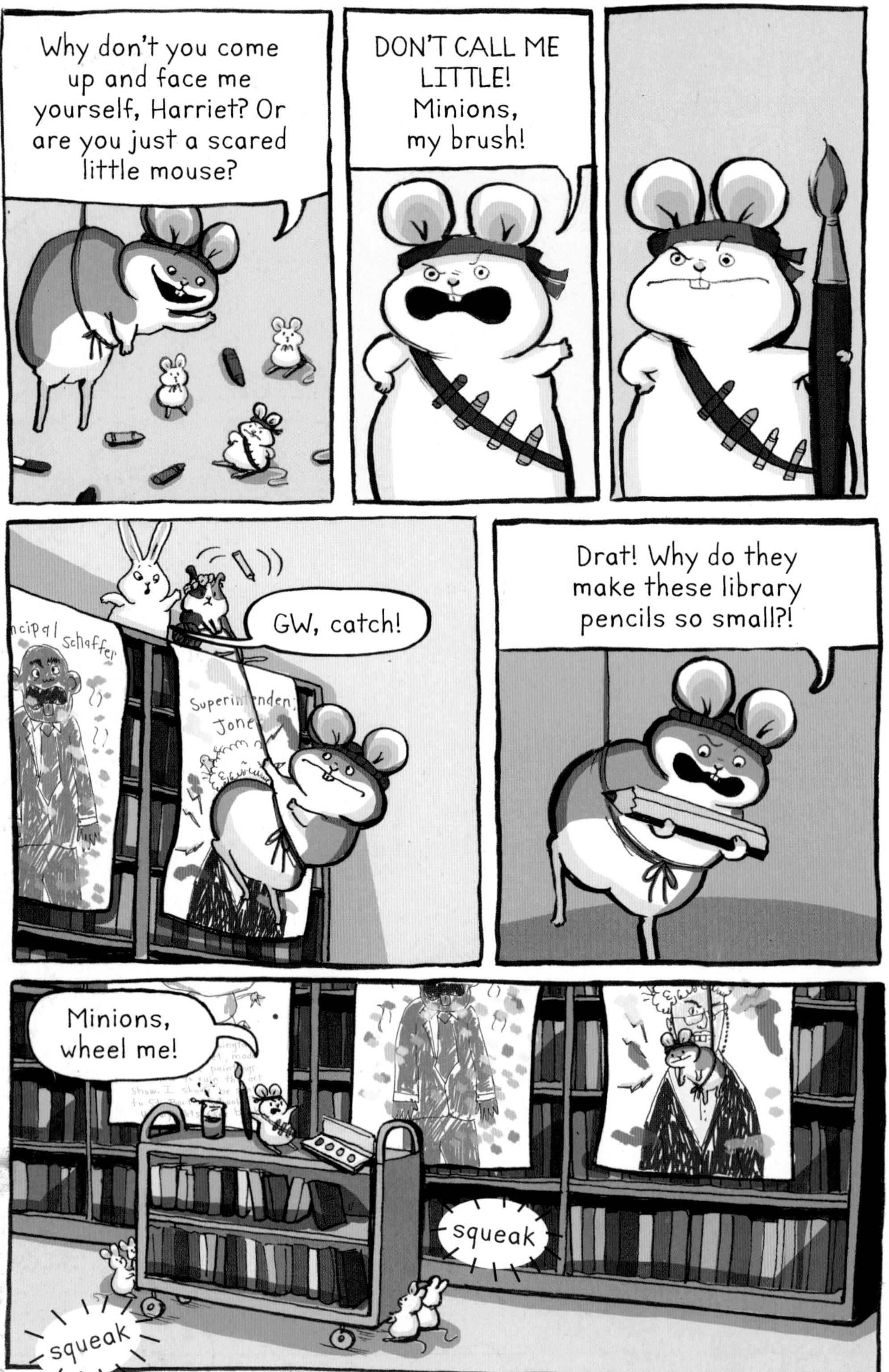
Why don't you come up and face me yourself, Harriet? Or are you just a scared little mouse?
DON'T CALL ME LITTLE! Minions, my brush!
GW, catch!
Drat! Why do they make these library pencils so small?!
Minions, wheel me!
squeak
squeak

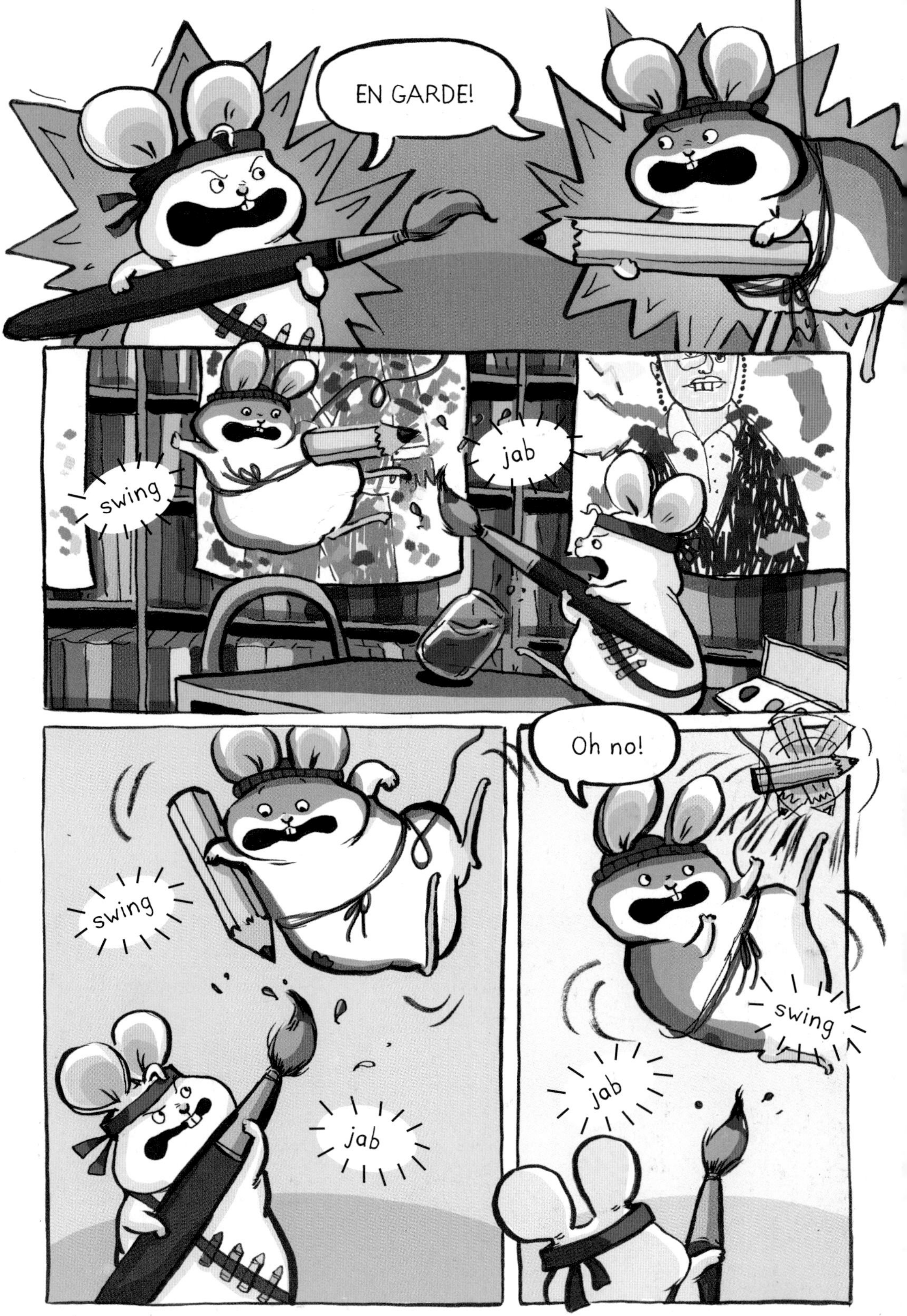
EN GARDE!
swing
jab
Oh no!
swing
jab
swing
jab

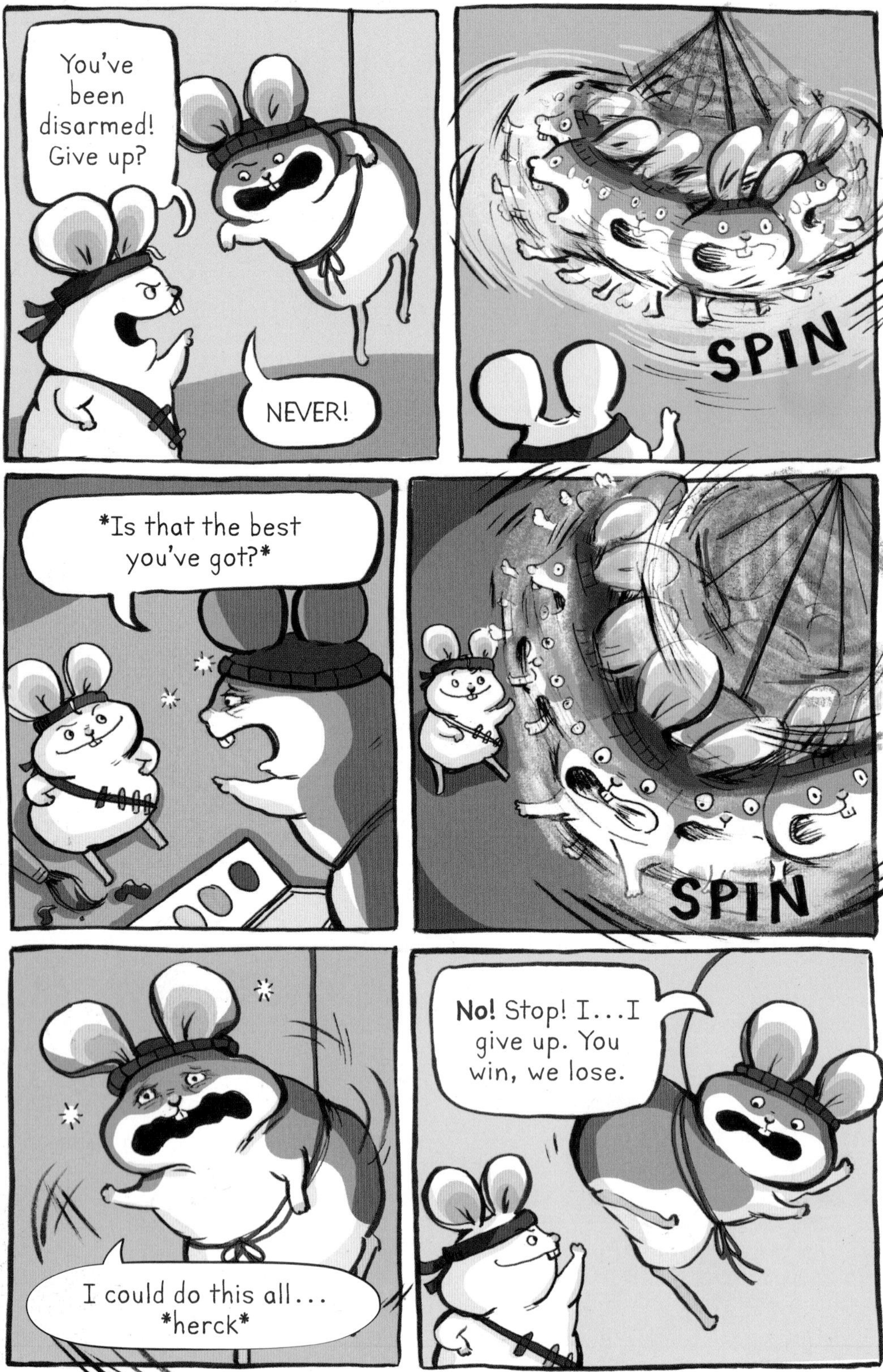
You've been disarmed! Give up?
NEVER!
SPIN
Is that the best you've got?
SPIN
I could do this all... *herck*
No! Stop! I...I give up. You win, we lose.

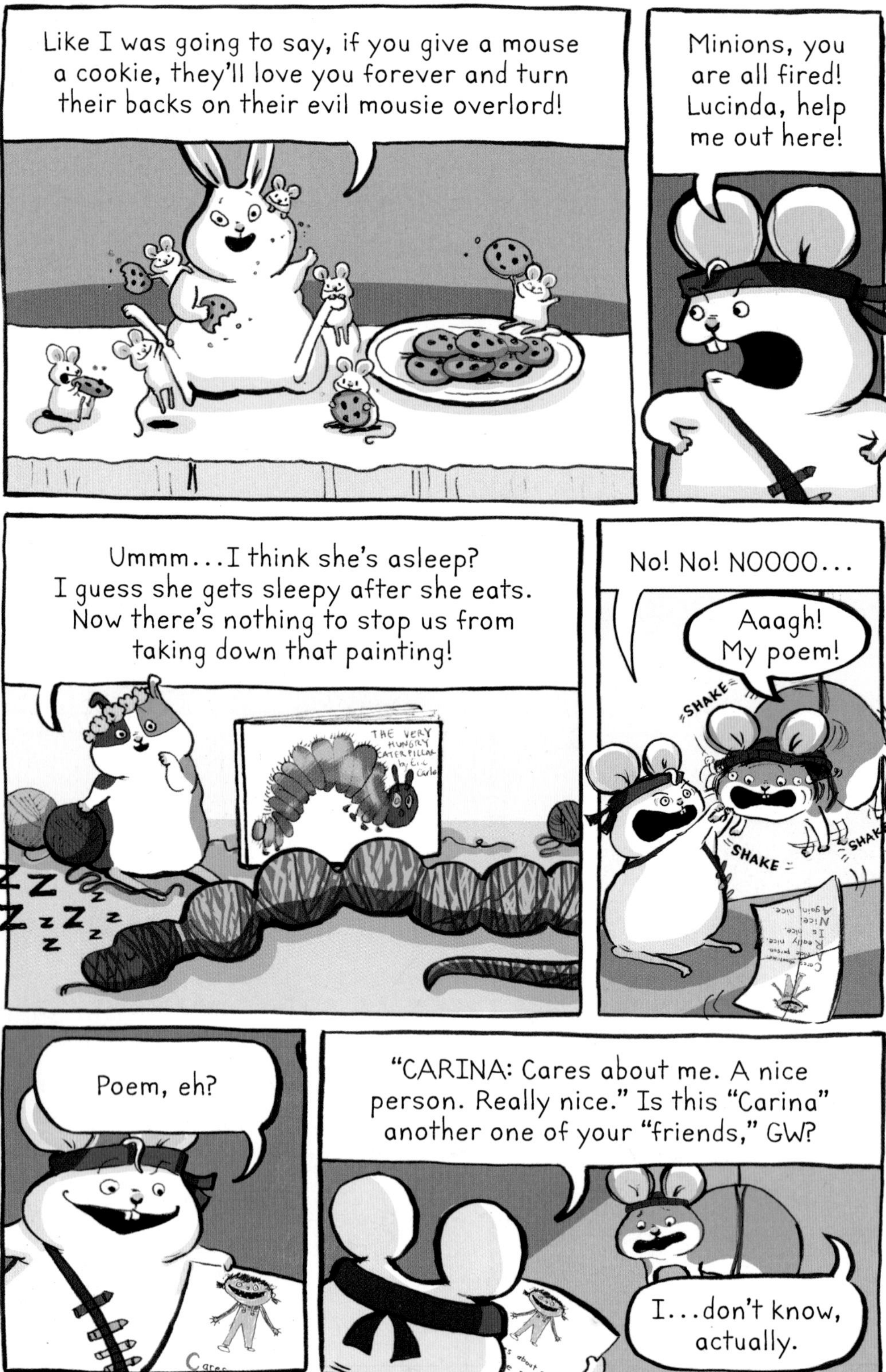

Like I was going to say, if you give a mouse a cookie, they'll love you forever and turn their backs on their evil mousie overlord!
Minions, you are all fired! Lucinda, help me out here!
Ummm...I think she's asleep? I guess she gets sleepy after she eats. Now there's nothing to stop us from taking down that painting!
THE VERY HUNGRY CATERPILLAR by Eric Carle
No! No! NOOOO...
Aaagh! My poem!
SHAKE
SHAKE
SHAKE
Poem, eh?
"CARINA: Cares about me. A nice person. Really nice." Is this "Carina" another one of your "friends," GW?
I...don't know, actually.

Chapter 10

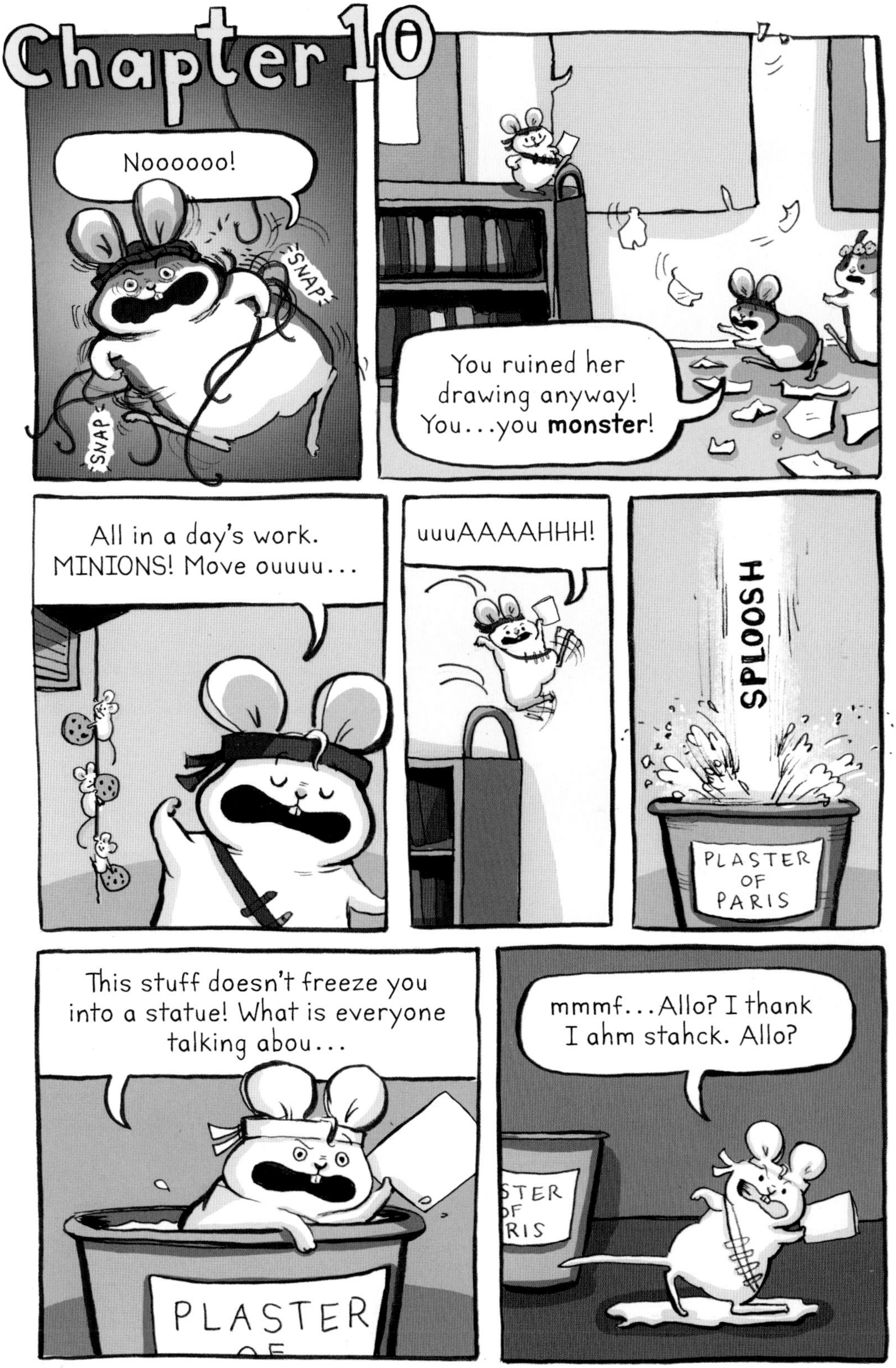

Noooooo!
SNAP
SNAP
You ruined her drawing anyway! You...you **monster**!
All in a day's work. MINIONS! Move ouuuu...
uuuAAAAHHH!
SPLOOSH
PLASTER OF PARIS
This stuff doesn't freeze you into a statue! What is everyone talking abou...
PLASTER OF
mmmf...Allo? I thank I ahm stahck. Allo?
STER OF RIS

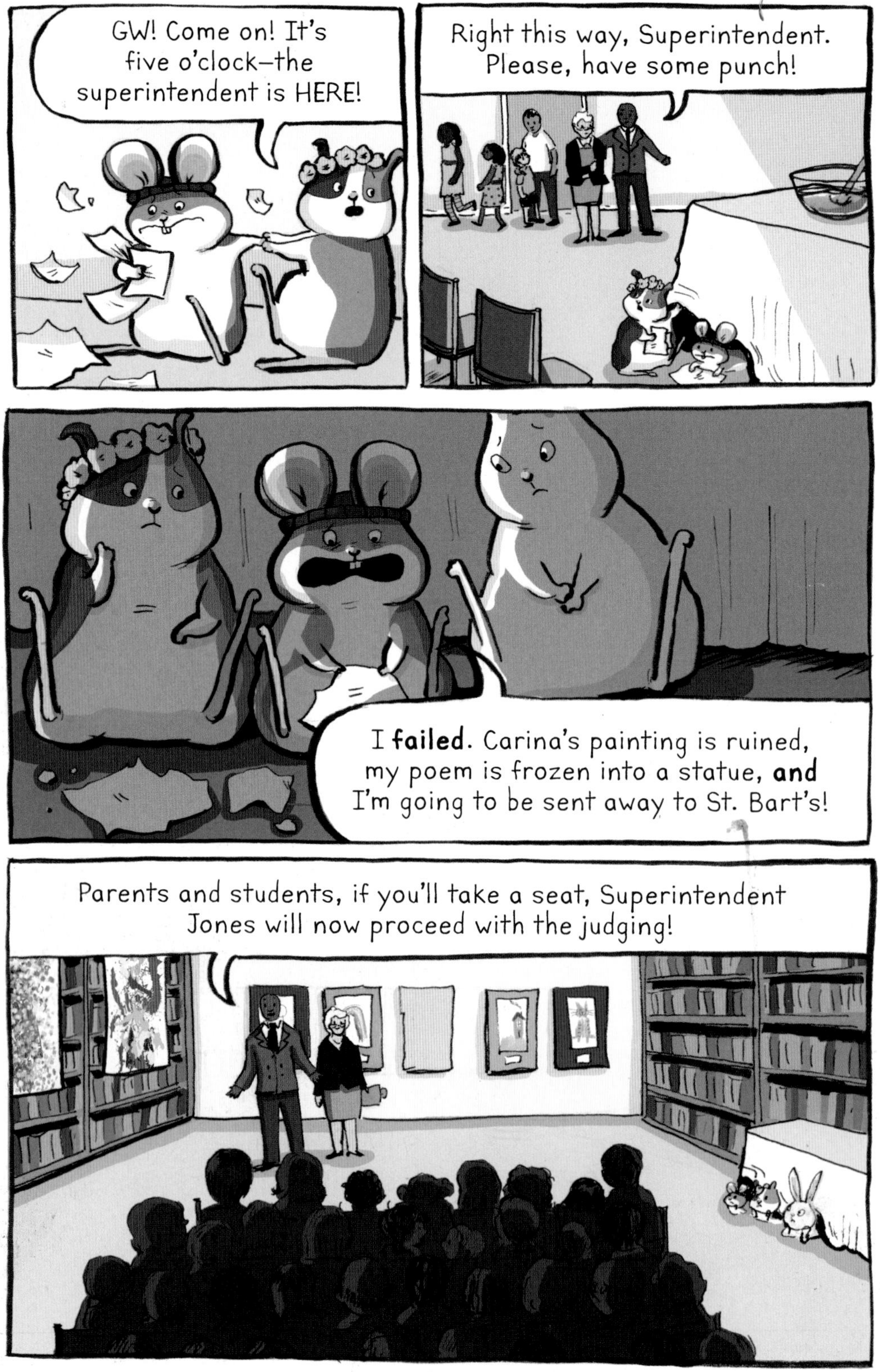
GW! Come on! It's five o'clock—the superintendent is HERE!
Right this way, Superintendent. Please, have some punch!
I **failed**. Carina's painting is ruined, my poem is frozen into a statue, **and** I'm going to be sent away to St. Bart's!
Parents and students, if you'll take a seat, Superintendent Jones will now proceed with the judging!

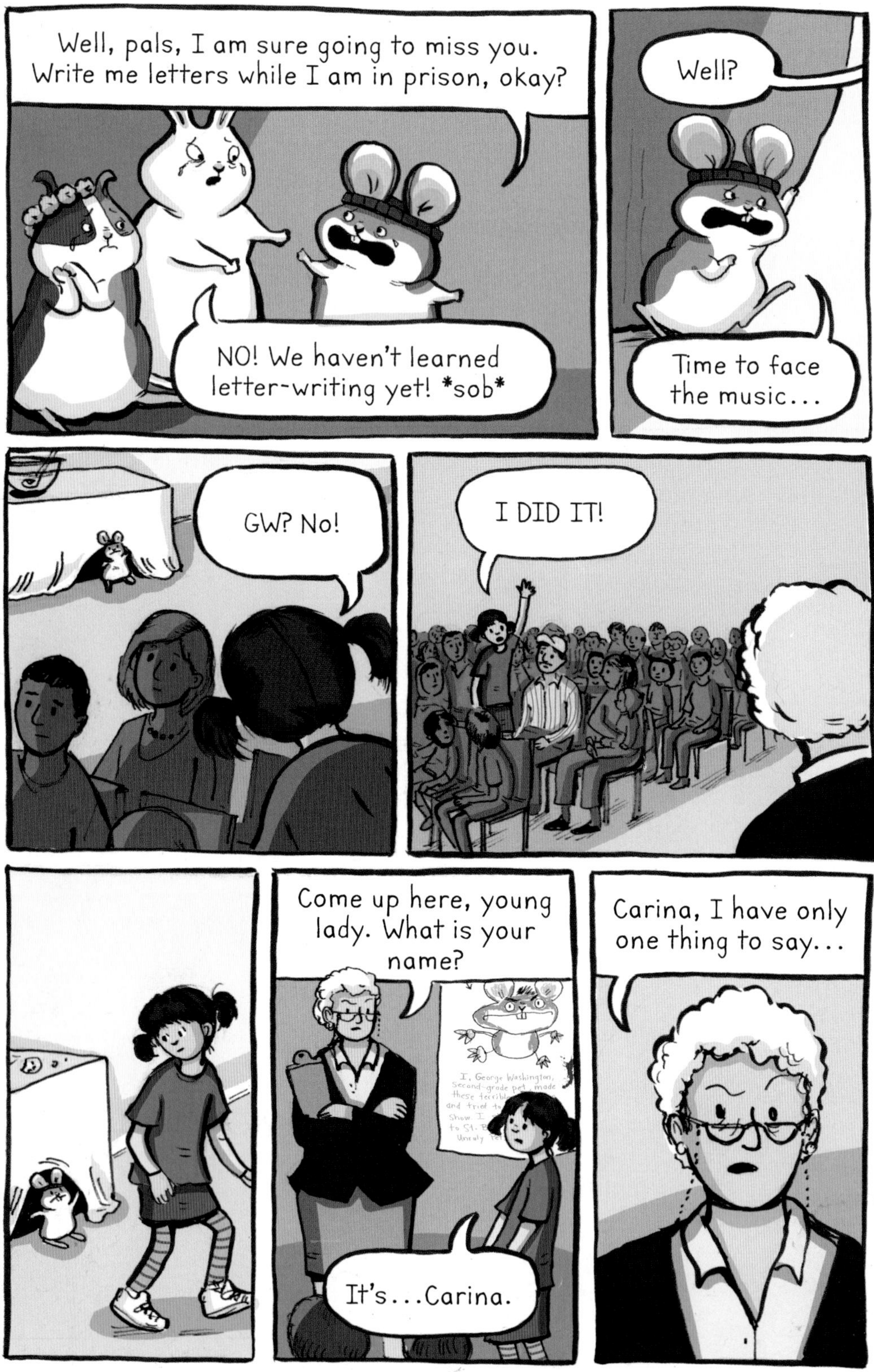
Well, pals, I am sure going to miss you. Write me letters while I am in prison, okay?
NO! We haven't learned letter-writing yet! *sob*
Well?
Time to face the music...
GW? No!
I DID IT!
Come up here, young lady. What is your name?
It's...Carina.
Carina, I have only one thing to say...

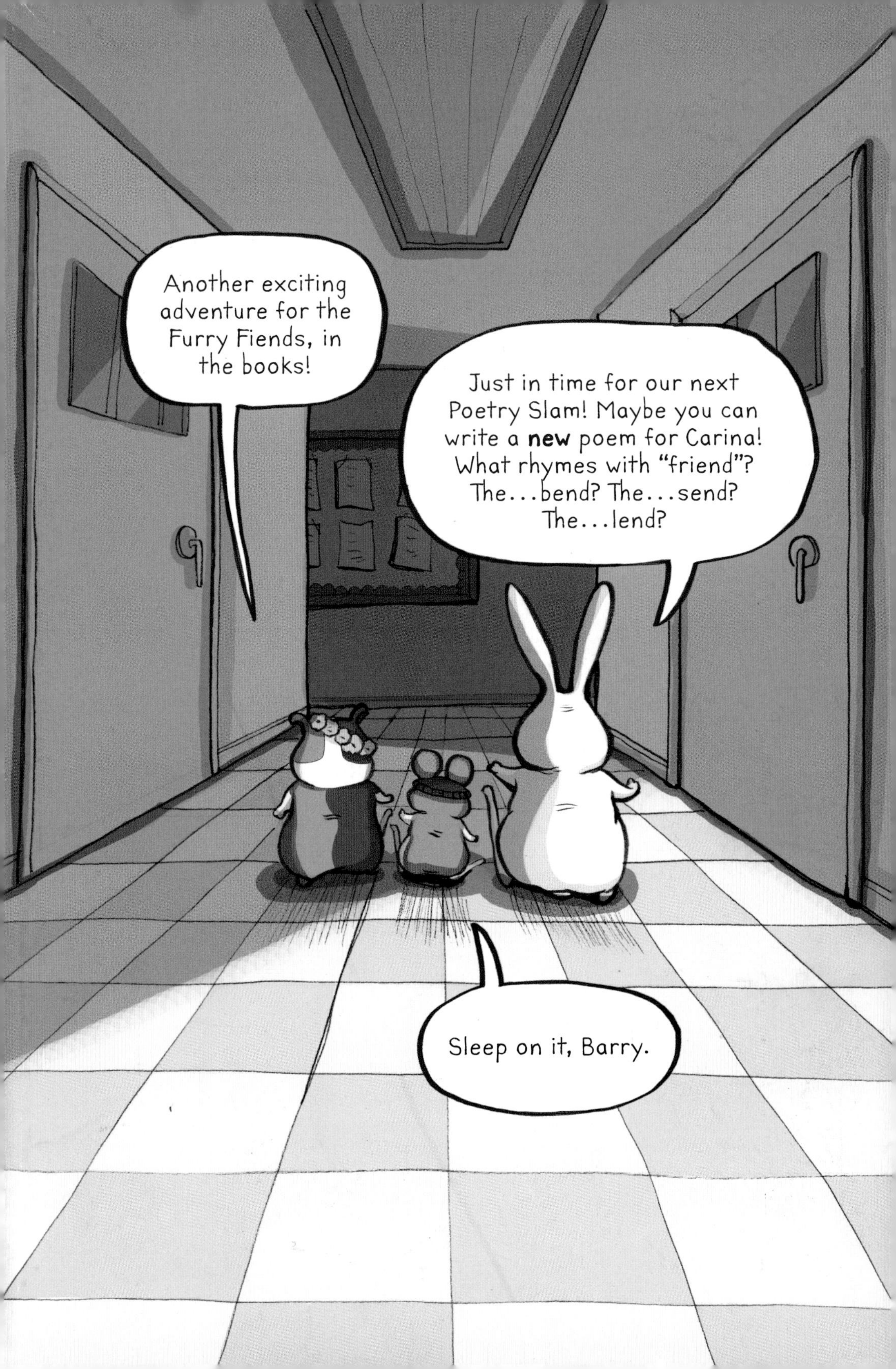
Another exciting adventure for the Furry Fiends, in the books!
Just in time for our next Poetry Slam! Maybe you can write a **new** poem for Carina! What rhymes with "friend"? The...bend? The...send? The...lend?
Sleep on it, Barry.

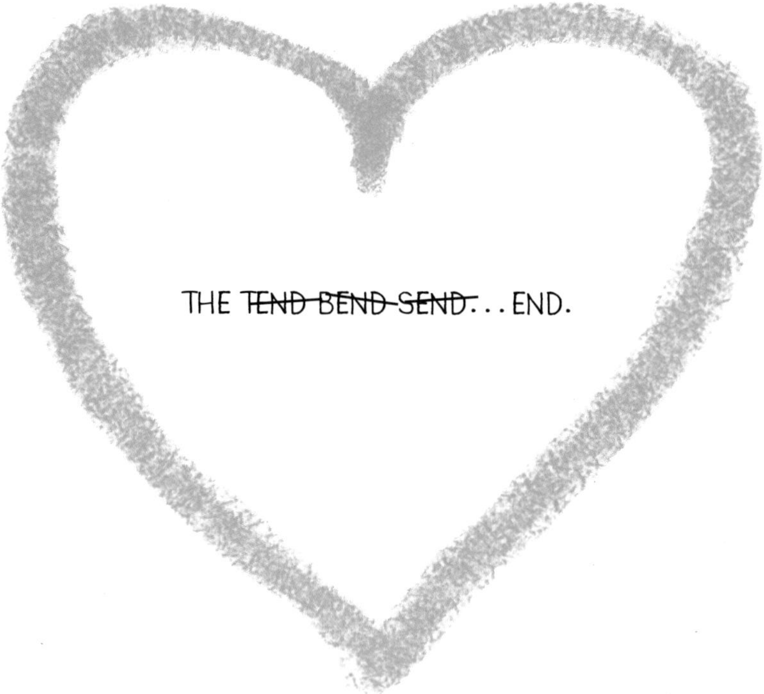
THE ~~TEND BEND SEND~~. . . END.

To Mom and Dad, for the inspiration.

Henry Holt and Company
Publishers since 1866
175 Fifth Avenue
New York, New York 10010
mackids.com

Library of Congress Control Number: 2016949882

ISBN (HC) 978-1-62779-118-2
1 3 5 7 9 10 8 6 4 2

ISBN (PB) 978-1-62779-119-9
1 3 5 7 9 10 8 6 4 2

Our books may be purchased in bulk for promotional, educational, or business use.
Please contact your local bookseller or the Macmillan Corporate and Premium Sales Department at (800) 221-7945 ext. 5442 or by e-mail at MacmillanSpecialMarkets@macmillan.com.

First Edition—2017
The artist used pen and ink with color added digitally to create the illustrations for this book.
Printed in China by Toppan Leefung Printing Ltd.,
Dongguan City, Guangdong Province

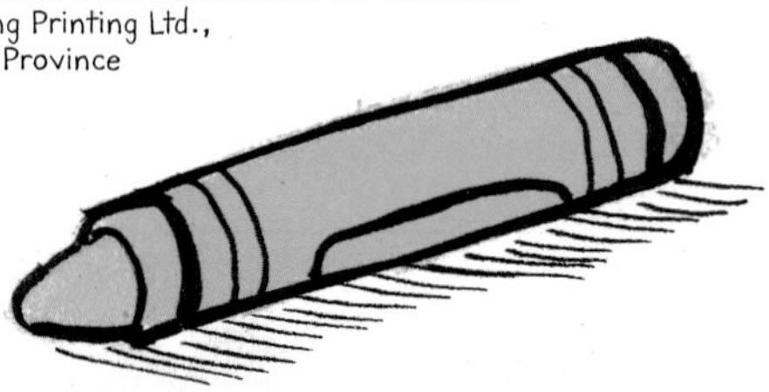